## THE MYSTERY OF THE AZTEC WARRIOR

The handwritten will of a deceased world-traveler is strange and mysterious. Its cryptic instructions are to deliver "the valuable Aztec warrior to the rightful owner, a descendant of an Aztec warrior." What is the valuable object and where is it? What is the name of the owner and where is he? Frank and Joe Hardy have only one slim clue to work with: the name of a complete stranger who can help find the answers.

Despite the harassments, the threats, and the attacks made upon them by an unknown, sinister gang, Frank and Joe unravel clue after clue in their adventure-packed search for the living descendant of the mighty Aztec nation which once ruled Mexico. The hunt leads to a market place in Mexico City, to the Pyramids at Teotihuacan, to the tombs of Oaxaca—where Chet Morton, the Hardys' pal, is nearly buried alive by foul play.

It takes as much high courage as clever deduction for the young detectives to defeat their ruthless foes and to decipher the fascinating secrets of the strange and mysterious will.

"We must get to that courtyard!" Frank yelled

*Hardy Boys Mystery Stories*

# THE MYSTERY OF THE AZTEC WARRIOR

BY

FRANKLIN W. DIXON

**GROSSET & DUNLAP**
A FILMWAYS COMPANY
Publishers • New York

ISBN: 0-448-08943-2 (TRADE EDITION)
ISBN: 0-448-18943-7 (LIBRARY EDITION)

## CONTENTS

# THE MYSTERY
## OF THE
# AZTEC WARRIOR

## CHAPTER I

## *The Injured Intruder*

FRANK and Joe Hardy followed their father into the law office of Otis Weaver, a Bayport attorney.

"Hello, Fenton!" said Mr. Weaver, getting up to shake hands with the tall, athletic-looking detective. "Frank—Joe—how are you?"

Tall, dark-haired Frank said, "We're fine and ready to tackle a case, Mr. Weaver."

His brother Joe, blond, seventeen, and a year younger, smiled in anticipation.

The four sat down. "I have a really mysterious one for you to solve," the short, balding lawyer began. "You probably read in the paper recently of the death of Mr. Jonathan Moore."

The three Hardys nodded, and the boys' father added, "He was a bachelor, I believe. Rather eccentric and not in town for very long periods."

"That's right," said the attorney. "He traveled a great deal. Mr. Moore had no relatives closer

1

than cousins. There are a number of beneficiaries mentioned in his will, but none of them can receive any money until a certain mystery is cleared up."

Mr. Weaver revealed that although Mr. Moore had handwritten his will, it was quite clear, and legally acceptable. There had been two witnesses.

"But these two men are deceased and therefore cannot answer any questions that might help to solve the mystery." The lawyer smiled. "I'm sure you three sleuths are eager to hear what the mystery is. I will read you certain paragraphs in the will."

From a drawer he pulled out a document and read: " 'I direct that the valuable Aztec warrior be given to the rightful owner, who claims to be a direct descendant of an Aztec warrior.' "

"Is that all?" Joe queried, as Mr. Weaver stopped speaking. "The person isn't named?"

"No," the lawyer answered. "There are two other notations which concern you three." He turned to the last sheet of the will and read aloud: " 'I direct that Fenton Hardy, detective of Bayport, and his sons Frank and Joe find the Aztec warrior and deliver his property to him. All expenses are to be paid from the corpus of my estate, and no monies are to be awarded to my beneficiaries until the Aztec warrior's property is returned to him.' "

Mr. Hardy asked that the two sections in the will be read again. After hearing them, he frowned, puzzled. "Have you any leads, Otis?"

"Not one. I've questioned each of the beneficiaries and other people who knew Mr. Moore, but none of them can offer a solution. There's one more item concerning you detectives. This sentence reads: 'The Hardys must find Roberto Hermosa.'"

Mr. Weaver handed a copy of the will to Mr. Hardy, asking if he would like to read it to see if there were any clue the lawyer had missed. The detective studied the document, then commented, "The rest of the will is quite clear. I'll just copy the parts which concern the boys and me."

While Mr. Hardy was busy writing in his notebook, Joe remarked, "Roberto Hermosa sounds Spanish. I wonder who he is."

"I don't know," Mr. Weaver said.

Frank asked the attorney if he had any idea what the Aztec warrior object was.

"No, none."

"Maybe it's a statue of an Aztec warrior," Joe remarked.

"There's none in Mr. Moore's house," the lawyer answered quickly.

"Could it be some kind of stuffed bird or animal?" Frank queried. "The winged serpent was sacred to the Aztecs."

"I didn't find any on the premises—or any

paintings of birds or animals," Mr. Weaver replied. "In fact, I didn't come across any object which might have even a remote connection with an Aztec warrior."

Mr. Hardy, recognizing an interesting challenge, said enthusiastically, "Otis, my sons and I will start working on the case very soon."

Frank and Joe were thrilled and asked if they might begin at once. Their father said he had an appointment and must leave.

"Suppose Frank and I go out to the Moore estate," Joe proposed. "Maybe if we look around the house we'll find a clue to the mysterious object."

The lawyer said he would take them. He drove out of town along a road where there had once been large estates which were now developments. He remarked that as soon as the Moore mystery was solved, the deceased man's property would be sold to a development company. "That will add a nice sum for the beneficiaries."

Presently Mr. Weaver turned into a driveway lined with stately old pine trees and pulled up to a large Victorian house, with grounds bordered by trim hedges. The lawyer parked the car and led the way up the high steps of the large porch. He unlocked the door, and the three entered.

The interior was attractive, with highly polished mahogany furniture. Heavy red draperies hung the full length of the living-room windows, which reached almost from ceiling to floor. A large desk stood at one end of the room just beyond an enormous stone fireplace.

"As you search for clues here," said Mr. Weaver, "you will find that this is typically a bachelor's home. Housekeepers whom Mr. Moore employed from time to time were not permitted to add any feminine touch to the furnishings."

Frank and Joe made a quick tour of the first floor to decide where to start their search for the Aztec warrior object. There were many objects standing on pedestals and on tables—gladiators, cowboys, and figures of athletes in action.

"Well, what do you think, boys?" asked Mr. Weaver, who had waited for them in the main hall. "I suppose you'll start tapping walls and—"

At that instant there was a terrific crash upstairs.

"What was that?" Frank asked.

"I have no idea," Mr. Weaver replied.

He and the boys dashed up the stairway, two steps at a time. Quickly they separated and looked in the various bedrooms. There was no sign of anything having fallen.

Mr. Weaver opened the door leading to the attic stairway and started up, with the boys crowding close on his heels. As they reached the attic, the three gasped. Amid a conglomerate of boxes and old furniture was a large mahogany bureau. It had fallen face forward.

*Pinioned underneath it was a man! He was struggling to free himself.*

"Wow!" Joe exclaimed, as he and Frank and Mr. Weaver dashed forward.

In a few moments they had raised the bureau to a standing position, then turned their attention to the thin, middle-aged man who had been caught under it. He had ceased to struggle and now lay on the floor, unconscious. He had a nasty gash on his head, was extremely pale, and his pulse rate was very slow.

"We'd better call an ambulance and have him taken to the hospital," Mr. Weaver spoke up. "I can't understand what he was doing here."

"Do you know who he is?" Joe asked.

"I think so," the lawyer replied. "We'll look for some identification to be sure." He opened the man's jacket and pulled a wallet from his pocket. "Yes, this is John Brower. He's one of the beneficiaries named in Mr. Moore's will."

"One of the beneficiaries!" Frank exclaimed. "He must have been looking for something special."

Mr. Weaver asked Joe to hurry downstairs and telephone for the ambulance. "We'd better not move Mr. Brower."

While he and Frank were waiting they kept close watch of the victim, but began to pull out the dresser drawers one by one to see what the man was after.

The man was struggling to free himself

"These certainly are stiff," Frank remarked. "Mr. Brower must have tried to open one and pulled the dresser over on himself."

"I'm afraid so," Mr. Weaver agreed. "He had no right being here. I wonder how he got in."

The drawers were filled with a collection of old books and old clothes. "Nothing unusual at all," Frank remarked. "I was hoping maybe we could find a clue to the Aztec warrior object."

Joe returned from the first floor and said the ambulance would be there in a few minutes. He went back downstairs to wait for it and in a very short time an intern and an attendant carrying a stretcher came up to the attic. The doctor examined Mr. Brower, then said, "This man must be taken to the hospital."

The two men transferred the patient to the stretcher, carried him downstairs and out to the ambulance, with the boys following. As soon as it had driven away, Frank said he would like to return to the attic and make a search.

"Mr. Brower may have had a good hunch. Also, I noticed several boxes of picture slides. Maybe there'll be a clue to our case in one of them!"

"Then let's go!" Joe urged.

# CHAPTER II

## An Attic Mishap

"You mean there might be a picture of the Aztec warrior among these slides?" Mr. Weaver asked, as he and the Hardys reached the attic.

"Yes, either of the man or of the object," Frank answered eagerly.

Mr. Weaver was intrigued by the idea and suggested that the three of them carry the boxes of slides downstairs. "When I was searching the house, I noticed a screen and projector on the first floor. By the way, only a few of the boxes are marked, so you'll probably have hundreds of pictures to look at."

Quickly they gathered up the boxes and began lugging them down the two flights of stairs. As Joe, in the lead, started for the first floor, he suddenly tripped on a worn spot in the carpeting. Two boxes flew from his arms, and he went sprawling.

Joe started to slide downward but caught a banister rail and pulled himself up, rubbing a bruised elbow. The slides lay in the hallway below, hopelessly mixed up.

"Great!" he said in chagrin.

Frank chuckled. "All in a sleuth's day."

The boys picked up the slides, and Mr. Weaver brought out the screen and projector.

While Joe set these up in the living room, Frank put aside the boxes on which there were notations of Greece, Italy, Egypt, and India. "I'm sure we won't find a picture of either Aztec warrior among these," he said. "I'll bet what we're looking for has something to do with Mexico."

The draperies were drawn, and Frank began handing slides from unmarked boxes to Joe. The first group of pictures looked as if they had been taken in the Rocky Mountains. Then came scenes in Hawaii, Canada, and England.

Although the boys had not yet come across any pictures of Mexico, they were so fascinated by the slides that they did not realize a full hour had gone by. Presently Mr. Weaver mentioned the time. "Two more boxes and we'll have to quit," he announced. "I must get back to the office."

Joe turned the projector to full speed, and the slides began flashing on and off the screen.

Suddenly Frank gave a shout. "We've hit Mexico! That's a building at the University in Mexico City!"

"You've been there?" Mr. Weaver asked him.

"Joe and I visited Mexico and once had a fleeting glimpse of Mexico City. But I recognized the university from pictures I've seen."

Joe then threw a slide on the screen which Mr. Weaver recognized as the Pyramid of the Sun, one of the great ruins outside Mexico City.

"Hold that picture!" Frank called out. "It's Aztec. There might be a clue in it."

The Hardys could not detect anything extraordinary. The few people in the picture were not distinct enough to be recognized.

Joe released the hold button, and the projector began to work automatically again. There were some pictures of candle cactus, and of a lake with fishermen who held strange-looking nets.

"That's Lake Patzcuaro," said Mr. Weaver. "Those are the butterfly nets. It's the only place in the world where fish nets like those are used. Well, boys, I must leave. We'll come back sometime and look at the rest of the slides."

"Would you mind if Joe and I stay here and finish them now?" Frank asked.

Mr. Weaver smiled. "Personally, no, but I have a responsibility as an executor, and such a thing might be criticized."

While he was talking, Joe showed one more

slide. It was a picture of two men standing side by side. Joe pushed the hold button.

"That one on the left is Mr. Moore!" the lawyer said excitedly.

"And the Indian-Spanish-looking gentleman with him?" Joe said. "Is he Roberto Hermosa?"

"I don't know," Mr. Weaver replied.

Frank was staring at the picture. "He just might be the direct descendant of the Aztec warrior!" he cried out.

Mr. Weaver was so excited he forgot all about leaving. Joe quickly ran through the rest of the slides in the box. Each one showed the same two men in various parts of a lovely garden.

"Mr. Weaver," said Frank, "since some of these slides are similar, would you let me take one and make a print from it?"

The lawyer considered the request, then finally consented.

Frank picked out the clearest view of Mr. Moore and his companion, put the slide in a handkerchief, and slipped it into a pocket.

The projector, screen, and boxes of slides were put away. Then the lawyer and the two young detectives left the house, locking the door. As soon as the boys reached home, they went to their workshop over the garage to make a print, which Frank later tucked into his wallet.

As the brothers were walking to the house, their father drove in. "Any luck?" he asked.

"We think we had a little," Frank told him, pulling out the picture. "One man is Mr. Moore. The other may be either Roberto Hermosa or the Aztec warrior descendant. We found the picture in a box of Mr. Moore's Mexican slides."

The three went into the comfortable, well-furnished house, where they were greeted by Mrs. Hardy. She was a small, slender woman with a sweet smile. She tried to take the adventuresome life of her family philosophically, but worried over the dangers she knew they encountered.

They were met also by Miss Gertrude Hardy, the detective's sister, who lived with them. She was a tall, spare woman, who adored her nephews, but frequently made it quite clear she thought they were not cautious enough in their sleuthing. Upon a few occasions her dire predictions of danger had come true.

Frank and Joe had been through many hair-raising adventures, starting with the mystery of *The Tower Treasure*. Recently they had solved a most unusual case, *The Viking Symbol Mystery*, in northwest Canada.

When Aunt Gertrude heard about the beneficiary who had been searching in the attic, she said tartly, "The idea! Why, he should be cut out of the will! There's no telling what he's already gotten away with!"

"We don't know that he was trying to steal anything," Frank defended Mr. Brower.

Aunt Gertrude was unconvinced. "There may be secret hiding places in that house," she declared. "If *I* were in Mr. Weaver's place, I'd get out a search warrant and go through all that Mr. Brower's effects."

Mr. Hardy patted his sister's shoulder. "I'm sure that the man will have a good explanation when he regains consciousness. Let's give him a chance to tell his story."

"This is your case, of course, but I wouldn't put too much faith in that man!" she said, and hurried to the kitchen. Mrs. Hardy waited with the boys while the detective telephoned the hospital. He reported to his family that Mr. Brower was still unconscious.

"He must have had a bad whack on the head," Mr. Hardy remarked.

Frank and Joe talked about the case until luncheon was ready. The meal included one of Aunt Gertrude's famous strawberry shortcakes topped with a sea of whipped cream. Presently the conversation turned again to the mystery.

"I think we should bone up on Mexican history," said Frank, "especially the period when the Aztecs were in power."

They excused themselves from the table and went to their father's library. Each boy selected a volume on Mexico's fascinating history.

"Whew! Human sacrifice!" Joe suddenly exclaimed. "They chose a young man, and for one year gave him the best food and clothes and entertainment possible, then killed him as a sacrifice to the war god!"

"Yes, and everything was done in the name of religion, with the priests as the killers!" Frank remarked.

The boys studied pictures of the elaborate costumes worn by Aztec warriors.

"Pretty fancy!" Joe remarked.

He pointed to a colorful illustration of a warrior in headdress and shirt of yellow parrot feathers and sprays of costly quetzal feathers, all decorated with gold. Another picture showed a whole squadron wearing uniforms made of jaguar skins and carrying shields adorned with golden disks, butterflies, and serpents; on their feet were embroidered sandals with thongs of orange leather.

The Hardys looked up as they heard a car roar up in front of the house and stop.

He grinned. 'I'll bet that's Chet!"

Joe peered from the window. "You're right."

Coming up the walk was a stout, good-natured-looking boy, a schoolmate of the Hardys. Chet Morton was a particular friend and often but unwittingly found himself involved in the mysteries the brothers were solving.

"Hi, fellows!" he said, as Joe opened the door and he walked in. "Why so glum?" he asked. "Something happen?"

"Oh, nothing much, except that we rescued an unconscious man, and we're searching for an Aztec warrior," Frank said nonchalantly.

Chet's eyes bulged. "You what!"

Quickly Frank and Joe told their friend the story of the Moore mystery. "Sounds crazy," Chet remarked. "But the part about Mexico interests me. I've read some of that history myself. Say, do you know what those old Aztecs used to eat?"

"No."

"They cooked with flowers," was Chet's surprising answer. "The acacia flower was supposed to cure melancholia. They sprinkled the flowers into an egg batter, fried it, and covered it with sugar and cinnamon." Chet smacked his lips. "I've always meant to try it."

"You suffering from melancholia?" Frank teased.

"Did they use any other kinds of flowers?" Joe asked.

"Sure. They made pie fillings with roses— boiled them up with sugar and lemon, and they made a drink out of the red blossoms from the Jamaica tree. You've heard of eating squash blossoms, haven't you? The Aztecs munched them during ceremonies to their rain-god."

Joe grinned. "I'm sure Aunt Gertrude would *love* to make some geranium soup!"

Chet laughed. "I just stopped by to ask you

fellows if you'd be interested in going to a movie. But now I suppose you'll have to stick around to solve this mystery."

"I'm afraid we will," Frank said. "But we'll be in touch!"

"Well, lots of luck to you," said Chet as he left the house. Frank and Joe watched him roar off down the street in his open jalopy. Then suddenly both brothers wanted to be on the move themselves.

"How about driving out to the Moore house tonight?" Joe proposed. "No restrictions on looking over the grounds."

"Sure thing."

After supper the boys took flashlights and set off in their car, with Frank at the wheel. When they reached the entrance to the Moore property, he stopped.

"Let's leave the car here," he suggested.

The boys hopped out and started up the driveway. It was still dusk, so there was no need for their flashlights. As they reached the left side of the house, the brothers were surprised to see a plump, white-haired woman standing there, gazing upward.

Hearing them, she turned. For a moment she looked hard at the boys, then smiled. "Good evenin'," she said. "You startled me. I thought maybe you were burglars. But you're nice-lookin' lads. My name is Mary O'Brien. I used to work by the day for the dear old gentleman who lived here."

"You mean Mr. Moore?" Frank asked her.

Mary O'Brien nodded. "It was sad, his death. Such a fine person. I enjoyed workin' for him. I was just relivin' those nice times."

Frank and Joe asked the woman if she had worked there recently. "Not for a couple of years," Mary O'Brien answered. "Lately Mr. Moore wasn't here much—he traveled a lot—so he didn't have any regular help."

"Miss O'Brien," said Frank, "did you ever hear Mr. Moore mention an Aztec warrior?"

A blank look came over the woman's face. "I never heard of such a thing."

"Mr. Moore traveled a lot in Mexico, didn't he?" Joe questioned.

"Oh my, yes—several times. He was a great one for bringin' back souvenirs from there."

"What did he do with them?" Frank queried.

"Well, some he kept and some he gave away."

The boys asked her if Mr. Moore had ever mentioned any friends in Mexico or people with whom he had traveled. Mary O'Brien shook her head. "To tell you the truth, Mr. Moore didn't talk a whole lot. He did say one time, though, that he was lookin' around Mexico for Indian weapons for his collection. A man traveled with him. But I'm sure he never mentioned his name."

"You say Mr. Moore had a collection of weapons?" Frank asked.

"He *did* have," Mary O'Brien answered. "He was talkin' about givin' the weapons to a museum. I wish you could've seen them. I used to have to dust every one, and some of the old pieces were pretty deadly lookin'."

"And you never heard Mr. Moore use the word 'Mexico' or 'Aztec' in connection with any of the weapons?" Joe questioned.

"No, he never did. The pieces came from Europe and Africa. Well, I got to be goin'. Good-by, boys."

The same thought was running through the minds of the brothers. Could the mysterious property of the Aztec warrior be some kind of weapon?

Frank and Joe walked silently across the lawn, past the front of the large house. As they looked down the right side of it, each gave a start.

A man, standing on a box, was trying to get into a first-floor window!

## CHAPTER III

# *A Mysterious Companion*

AT ONCE Frank and Joe sped toward the intruder. Unfortunately, the stranger spotted the Hardys. Jumping quickly from the box, he picked up a rock and threw it at the boys. Then he turned in the opposite direction and fled. The boys dodged the rock.

"Stop!" Joe yelled, although he knew the command was useless.

The brothers turned on their flashlights and dashed after the short, dark-haired figure, but he apparently was familiar with a rear exit from the grounds and disappeared among the shadows. Frank and Joe searched thoroughly, but the beams revealed only a series of dim footprints which faded out on a concrete path.

"I suppose we should report this," said Frank as they gave up the chase. "I'll stay here and keep watch. Joe, you go and phone the police."

Soon two officers arrived in a patrol car and examined the area where the intruder had been. They lifted fingerprints which the man had left on the window sill and said they would take along the box with the shoe prints on it.

"Thanks for the tip, boys," the driver of the patrol car said as the officers started away. "If you see any more burglars, let us know."

After the men had gone, Frank and Joe began their search for possible clues to the Aztec mystery. Beaming their flashlights around, they looked for some time with no success.

Then suddenly Frank exclaimed, "I think I've found something!"

Joe ran to his brother's side as Frank focused his light on a large tree. Crudely carved into the trunk were the head and shoulders of an Indian.

"It's hard to tell what he represents," Frank remarked, "but he could be an Aztec warrior."

The boys examined the whole tree trunk, looking for more clues. Another carving? A hollow spot? Nothing came to light.

"Maybe something is buried in the ground near here," Joe suggested.

There seemed to be no place within a radius of five feet of the tree trunk which looked as if it had been dug up. The ground was level, and the grass was the same color and texture as the surrounding area.

"If something's buried here we can't dig it up

tonight," Frank said practically. "Let's get Mr. Weaver's permission to do some digging here in the morning."

"I'm with you," his brother said.

Frank and Joe returned home and reported their discovery to Mr. Hardy, telling about the collection of weapons.

"That's very interesting," the detective said. "I'll ask Mr. Weaver about it. And I agree with you there's a good possibility an object is buried near the tree."

He phoned Mr. Weaver, who consented to having the area spaded up. He said he would meet the Hardys at the Moore estate about nine the next morning.

In answer to a question about the weapons collection, the lawyer said, "Mr. Moore gave it away a year ago. I came across the list of items. None of them had anything to do with the Aztecs."

As soon as Mr. Weaver and the Hardys arrived at the Moore estate the next day, Mr. Weaver produced spades, a shovel, and pickax from the garage. During the next hour, sod was carefully lifted, then deep holes were made in the ground. There were no signs of anything having been buried. Disappointed, Frank and Joe filled in the holes and patted the squares of sod back into place, got the garden hose, and sprinkled the grass generously.

Mr. Hardy said, "Otis, if you can take the time,

I'd like to go into the house and search through Mr. Moore's letters for clues to both Aztec warriors."

The attorney consented, saying he would help, although Mr. Moore's more recent correspondence had already been read.

Frank asked, "How about Joe and me looking through some more of those slides?"

"Good idea," said Mr. Weaver. "By the way, the police told me this morning that the fingerprints of that would-be intruder last night aren't on record, so he's not a previous offender as far as they can ascertain."

"And how about Mr. Brower—has he regained consciousness?" Frank asked.

"Not yet," replied Mr. Weaver, unlocking the house. "But his condition is better, and the doctors expect him to become conscious soon."

The boys hurried inside. They immediately set up the projector and screen and brought out more boxes of slides. It was some time before they came across a second box of Mexican pictures, but in a few minutes Joe exclaimed excitedly:

"Here's a real clue!"

The picture had been taken in front of a pyramid and showed the mysterious companion of Mr. Moore in the full costume of an ancient warrior.

"Hold everything until I get Dad and Mr. Weaver!" Frank said.

He ran off to the library, where the men were going through old letters and memorandums, and asked them to come look at the picture.

"Hmm!" said the detective, after seeing it. "I believe this is an excellent lead. The man in the picture may well be the one Mr. Moore referred to as the Aztec warrior."

"And is the rightful owner of the property we can't find," Mr. Weaver added.

"Who is he?" Frank asked. "Roberto Hermosa or someone else?"

"I'm sure this settles one thing," Joe spoke up, "and that is, the person we're trying to find is definitely in Mexico."

Mr. Hardy smiled. "Come now, Joe. Don't jump to conclusions. It does seem likely the man is in Mexico, but he might only have been visiting there."

Mr. Weaver pointed out that even if this were the man they were looking for, there was nothing in the picture to indicate what the property was which should be returned to him.

"What I can't understand," the lawyer added, "is why Mr. Moore put this whole stipulation in his will without giving the name of the owner."

"And why hold up payments to the beneficiaries until the mystery is solved?" Mr. Hardy asked.

Frank remarked, "Mr. Moore might have been

trying to protect both the owner and his possession for some special reason."

"You have a point there," said Mr. Weaver. "But what was the reason?"

"If it's something very valuable," Joe remarked, "Mr. Moore may have been trying to keep thieves from knowing about the Aztec warrior object."

"Then we'd better watch *our* step," Mr. Hardy commented.

The hunt for clues proceeded. The men went on with their search among the letters, and the boys continued to look at slide after slide. They came across a picture of the mysterious man alongside a tremendous tree. Printed on the slide were the words: TULE TREE AT MITLA.

"Wow! I never saw such a big tree trunk!" Joe exclaimed.

A few minutes later they came to another picture marked: ZÓCALO AT TAXCO.

"Here's our friend again!" said Frank, as the familiar figure was shown on the screen.

When Mr. Hardy and Mr. Weaver returned to the room, the boys showed them the two slides.

The detective rubbed his chin thoughtfully. "I feel pretty sure we'll find the man in these pictures in Mexico."

Frank and Joe watched their father's face as he gazed off into space. What was going through his mind? Suddenly he turned to his sons. "Boys, I believe that you and I had better divide up work on this case. I can't get away from here right now because of other commitments. How about you fellows going to Mexico and seeing if you can locate Roberto Hermosa?"

Joe grinned. "I could be ready to leave in an hour," he said. "And boy, what a trip!"

"You just buy my plane ticket, Dad," said Frank, "and I'll be on my way!"

Mr. Hardy smiled. "It won't be that easy. There's a ruling against teen-agers going around Mexico without an adult. I'll have to arrange for special passes for two young detectives on a worthwhile mission."

As Mr. Hardy stopped speaking, Mr. Weaver clapped him on the shoulder. "Fenton, that's a brilliant idea. You and I will keep on hunting around here for the Aztec warrior property. It will be kind of a race to see which half of this team comes out ahead."

Mr. Hardy laughed, then said to Frank and Joe, "How would you like to take Chet Morton along?"

"You mean it!" the boys exclaimed together.

Their father nodded. "He'll hold you down if you get too fool-HARDY!"

The brothers grinned. Then Frank asked Mr. Weaver if he might take the slides showing the mysterious man and make prints of them. The lawyer consented. The boys hurried home. After lunch, Joe went to the workshop to make the prints, while Frank telephoned Chet. There was a war whoop from the other end of the line.

"Hot tamales!" Chet exclaimed. "I can have all of them I want!"

"How about coming over so we can talk about our trip?" Frank asked.

"Be right there," Chet promised.

"Meet you out in our workshop," said Frank.

Fifteen minutes later the boys heard the sound of a familiar horn. Instead of a few blasts, the raucous noise continued.

"Chet sure is happy!" said Joe with a grin. "Well, we may as well go out and welcome him!"

Standing at the curb was Chet's jalopy, its horn still blowing continuously. The stout boy was not inside the car. He was standing on the sidewalk, his face red with embarrassment.

Aunt Gertrude was there, wagging a finger at him and saying, "The idea! If you don't know how to take care of a car, you have no business running one!"

By this time several neighbors had come rushing toward the jalopy. One woman called out, "Is something the matter at your house, Miss Hardy?"

Frank and Joe howled with laughter as they hurried toward the scene.

# CHAPTER IV

## *The Hijacked Plane*

FRANK waved at the crowd gathered near Chet's jalopy. "Nothing's wrong here except a little short in the horn-button wiring," he said.

Joe quickly released the car hood and disconnected a wire. The horn stopped blowing.

"What'll I do now if I want to use it?" Chet asked, dismayed, as the onlookers dispersed.

"Just get the wire replaced," said Joe.

Chet scratched his head. "I haven't many spare parts, but I do have some extra wire!"

"Get to it, boy," said Joe. "Unless you want us to send for a mechanic!"

"Okay, okay," Chet agreed. He found a pair of pliers in the dashboard compartment and went to work. With Frank and Joe's help he soon had the old wire replaced and the horn in proper working order.

"Thanks, fellows," he said. "I didn't mean to

hold up your plans. Tell me about this Mexican trip. I can't wait to go."

First they gave Chet some kidding advice about eating in Mexico. "You'll have to be careful," Frank told him, "or you'll burn up your insides."

"Oh, all their food isn't hot," Chet retorted. "*Tortillas* and *enchiladas* are mighty good eating, but no red pepper chocolate sauce for me."

Joe chanted in a singsong, off-key voice:

"For making *tortillas* you'll use a *metate*.
And for a bed we'll use a *petate*."

Chet scowled. "You won't catch me sleeping on any straw mat. I'm not an Aztec!"

Frank and Joe laughed, then led the way into the house to brief Chet on the trip and show him the prints. "We're going to the various places where Mr. Moore took pictures," Frank told him.

"That means we'll see some Indian ruins?"

"We sure will—probably several of them."

Chet looked dubious. "I hope you won't ask me to climb to the top and look for clues. I hear those steps are so narrow you have to walk sideways to keep from falling off."

"Right," said Frank. "That's the best way to go either up or down, according to the Indians. You zigzag from left to right, so you never get tired or out of breath."

Shortly afterward, Mr. Hardy came in to announce that all the arrangements for the trip had been made. "I have the special passes for you three teen-agers and have reserved hotel accommodations in Mexico City. If there are any other places you want to investigate, you'll have to make your own plans."

"How are we going to travel?" Chet asked.

"In my plane," the detective answered. "Jack Wayne will take you and then return immediately. He'll fly down for you when you're ready to come back."

Mr. Hardy had found it necessary to purchase a plane for use in emergencies connected with his work. Both Frank and Joe had piloted the craft, but Jack Wayne was always in command on long trips.

"When do we start?" Joe asked.

"How about tomorrow morning?"

The three boys said they would be ready, and Chet left to go home and pack. Frank busied himself working out an itinerary of the places shown in Mr. Moore's pictures. Joe went to the workshop to print extra copies of the deceased man's mysterious companion.

When this was done, the brothers drove to the airfield to check out the Hardy plane. Jack Wayne was not there, so the boys hopped into the blue-and-white, single-engine craft and Frank took the controls. Soon they were soaring above Bayport, then out over Barmet Bay.

"Seems to be shipshape," Frank observed, circling back.

As they prepared to land, Joe suddenly gasped in horror. "Look out!"

Zooming directly toward them was another plane! There was not a second to lose. Frank pulled back on the stick and sent his craft sharply upward. A collision was avoided by mere yards as the other plane sped on below them.

The Hardys shuddered at the close call. "That pilot must be nuts!" Joe said hoarsely.

Frank landed without further incident. From the tower they learned that a novice had been flying the other plane, and had temporarily "frozen" in panic.

"Too bad," said Joe. "He'd better stay grounded for a while."

Still shaken, the boys went home. As they entered the hall, their father was answering the phone. Mr. Weaver was calling to say that Mr. Brower had regained consciousness. Could the three detectives come to the Bayport Hospital?

"Right away," Mr. Hardy promised.

The three went to the hospital. After inquiring at the Information Desk where Mr. Brower's room was, they took the elevator to the second floor. Mr. Weaver greeted them at the door of the patient's room.

Although somewhat pale, Mr. Brower managed

an apologetic smile. "I am sorry I put you boys to so much trouble. I was very foolish and regret having entered the house. Jonathan gave me a key years ago that I never returned."

Mr. Brower added that he was badly in need of the inheritance willed to him. "I was merely doing what you people are—looking for a clue to the Aztec warrior object."

"By finding it, you could receive your inheritance sooner," Mr. Hardy remarked.

"That's right. Well, I didn't have any luck and did have a bad accident for my trouble."

Mr. Hardy asked Mr. Brower if he had any idea what the Aztec warrior object was. The sick man shook his head. "Jonathan told me a long time ago that he had received a very unusual and valuable piece from a descendant of the Aztecs, but he never told me what it was. My cousin was pretty secretive."

"And *you* have no idea what this thing was?"

"Not the slightest."

Mr. Brower said that his cousin had told him the precious piece had been lent to him on condition that he return it at the end of five years. "He may have meant the Aztec warrior object mentioned in the will."

"Then it's possible this mysterious piece may have been sent back already and Mr. Moore forgot to take the notation out of the will," Mr. Weaver suggested

Mr. Brower said he doubted this. "Only three years have gone by since Jonathan received it. My cousin said he had the object safely hidden. I have assumed it is in his house."

Since nothing more could be learned from Mr. Brower, his visitors left. When they reached the street, Frank suggested that they all return to the Moore home and make a still more intensive search. The others agreed and soon the lawyer was unlocking the front door of the mansion.

Mr. Hardy, who always carried several detecting devices in the trunk of his car, went to get them.

The boys helped to carry in a portable fluoroscope and a metal detector. Every wall, floor, and ceiling was gone over. Several times Frank and Joe became excited as the fluoroscope lighted up objects or the detector began to click, but nothing of importance was located. The Hardys had no better luck with a systematic examination for hollow walls and trap doors. Nothing was found.

Mr. Weaver, who had followed the Hardys around in amazement, sighed. "The answer to this whole mystery must lie with Roberto Hermosa."

Mr. Hardy agreed that they seemed to have come to a dead end in every other direction. He asked if there had been any late word on the man who had tried to get into the house.

"No," Mr. Weaver replied. "Just to be sure

the fellow wasn't one of the beneficiaries, I checked each one. Every man has an alibi." The lawyer smiled. "I tried hard to be a detective but haven't come up with a single clue."

"I think you have done very well for an amateur," said Mr. Hardy with a smile. "Here we are, trained in this kind of work, and we haven't done any better than you!"

When they reached Mr. Weaver's office, the lawyer got out of the car and wished the boys the best of luck in Mexico. "It has just about everything one could wish in the way of scenery, the mystery of ancient civilizations, and the fascinating Spanish influence."

Joe grinned. "We'll try to take in all of them, and solve your mystery besides."

When the Hardys reached home, the boys' mother greeted them in Spanish, adding, "I thought I might as well give you a little practice."

Frank and Joe were amazed at their mother's command of the language, which they and Chet already spoke.

"I thought I'd surprise you," she said. "I'll tell you a little secret. I studied Spanish in school but forgot most of what I learned, so I have been taking lessons for the past two months."

"Mother, why don't you come along with us?" Frank asked suddenly.

Mrs. Hardy smiled. "I don't think I'd be equal to meeting an Aztec warrior!"

The Hardys spent a pleasant evening together. The following morning Chet's father dropped his son off at the Hardy home. With warm embraces from Mrs. Hardy for Frank and Joe, and words of advice from Aunt Gertrude to watch out for jaguars, the three boys set off for the airport with Mr. Hardy.

As they drove along the road toward the terminal, Joe exclaimed, "Isn't that your plane, Dad, way over on that last runway?"

"Yes, it is. I guess Jack will taxi up. We're a little early."

The detective let the boys out, since he had an early appointment. He said good-by and called after them, "I hope to see you soon with the mystery solved!"

The three young travelers walked through the administration building and out to the area where private planes taxied up to take on passengers. The Hardy plane was still at the far end of the runway. Suddenly it began to move, but instead of taxiing toward the boys, it gathered speed, rolled down the runway, and in a few moments was airborne.

"Say, what's going on here?" Frank asked. "Jack Wayne wouldn't take off without us!"

"You bet he wouldn't!" Joe cried excitedly. "Something sure is going on! Our plane has been hijacked!"

# CHAPTER V

## *The Tattoo*

"WHAT do you mean your plane's been hijacked?" Chet Morton asked unbelievingly.

"Just that!" Joe answered.

"I'm afraid he's right," Frank added, starting to run toward the administration building. "We must talk to the tower right away!"

The report from the tower was even more disturbing. Jack Wayne himself was at the controls and had asked for immediate clearance. Frank quickly told his story, and the dispatcher said he would do all he could to bring back the Hardy plane.

The boys paced anxiously while awaiting word. Presently they were informed that there was no response to calls to the aircraft.

"Must be a hijacking," the tower dispatcher said. "I'll report this to the FAA."

Frank and Joe told the dispatcher that they would get in touch with the police, then do some investigating at the field to see what they could learn. Their sleuthing revealed little that they did not already know.

Several mechanics had seen Jack Wayne and even spotted him getting into the Hardy plane. They had not observed anyone going aboard with him, but they had noticed a stranger talking to him on the field.

"What did this stranger look like?" Frank asked one of the mechanics.

"I can't tell you much. He was rather short and dark. To tell you the truth, he was too far away for me to make out any details. I sure am sorry to hear what happened and hope you get your plane back soon." The man returned to his work on the landing gear of a jetliner.

As the boys walked away, Joe said, "I'll bet that stranger is connected with our mystery—he might even be the one we chased away from the Moore house—and forced Jack to get clearance for a take-off."

"Let's go to the tower and find out what's doing," Frank suggested.

The dispatcher greeted the boys with a worried look. "There's no trace of your plane, fellows. All the big airports have been notified. They haven't been in contact with your plane."

Because the dispatcher was extremely busy, the

three boys went back to the waiting room to discuss the unexpected situation.

"Do you know what this means?" Joe pointed out. "A kidnapping as well as a hijacking."

Chet's usually smiling face was glum. "I sure hope Jack doesn't get hurt. He's too swell a guy. The thing I can't figure is, what does the kidnapper hope to accomplish?"

"I guess if we knew the answer to that," said Frank, "we'd have a clue on how to trace Jack and the plane."

Chet wanted to know what the boys were going to do. "Give up the trip?"

The Hardys shook their heads vehemently. "Not on your life!" Joe said firmly.

Frank decided to get in touch with Mr. Hardy. He telephoned home, but the detective was not there. Mrs. Hardy, who had answered, was alarmed by what had happened and said she would call several places where she thought her husband was going to stop.

"You boys wait at the airport, and I'll have him get in touch with you there if I can find him."

They chafed under the delay. All three tried to pass the time by reading newspapers, but the words seemed meaningless as their thoughts reverted to the missing plane and pilot.

Finally Frank announced that he was going to call Mr. Weaver, saying it was just possible he might have some lead to offer. The lawyer was astounded at the story, and could offer no clue.

"Do you suppose," Frank asked, "that the man who tried to break into the Moore house could also be the hijacker?"

"That's very possible," Mr. Weaver conceded. "But we don't know anything about him."

"That's right, except Joe and I *did* catch a glimpse of him," Frank said. "That, together with a set of his fingerprints and shoe prints, may help to locate the man."

When Frank returned to the waiting room, he was delighted to find his father there. Mr. Hardy was greatly troubled by the news and concerned for Jack Wayne's safety. He expressed the opinion that it would be difficult to locate the hijacked plane. "No hijacker would dare land at a big airport where he would be arrested immediately. He'll probably come down at some farm or uncontrolled airfield.

"Personally," added Mr. Hardy, "I believe someone else is trying to locate the Aztec warrior. Apparently he is trying to scare you, thinking you'll give up the case and not go to Mexico to search for the warrior."

Joe, restless, was pacing back and forth as his father talked. "If that's the case," he said, "why don't we take one of the commercial flights to Mexico?"

His father's blue eyes twinkled. "That's just what I was going to suggest."

Frank sped to the reservations counter. By the time the others reached him, he had learned that the boys could obtain reservations on a late-night flight from New York City to Mexico City. "We'll have to take a plane out of here and change at Idlewild Airport."

The boys, eager to start the journey, decided to leave on the next plane to New York and spend a little time looking around the immense New York City air terminal.

"All right," said Mr. Hardy, and purchased three tickets.

When the boys arrived at Idlewild, Frank and Joe watched the incoming and outgoing airliners from one of the observation decks. Chet, declaring he was hungry, had gone to a snack bar.

Suddenly Frank grabbed Joe's arm. "Look at that mechanic down there!" he cried excitedly.

"What about him?" Joe asked.

Instead of answering, Frank started to run from the deck and down the stairs with Joe following, perplexed. They dashed through a corridor until they came to a gate near where the man was standing. "We're detectives!" said Frank to the guard. "Please let us go out and talk to that mechanic with the tattoo!"

The guard looked at them and at first was not inclined to grant their request. But apparently the boys' honest faces convinced him that they were telling the truth, and he let them through the gate. The mechanic was nearing the building and now Joe could see why his brother had been so excited.

*The man's sleeves were rolled up. On his left arm was a tattoo of an Aztec warrior!*

"And the fellow looks like an Indian!" Joe thought.

The Hardys stopped him, and Frank asked about the tattoo. The man laughed and said in English, with a Spanish accent, "I had this put on because I am direct descendant of an Aztec warrior."

Frank and Joe were almost speechless with astonishment. Had their quest for a direct descendant of an Aztec warrior come to an end? Was this the person to whom the valuable object belonged? Frank asked the mechanic if he knew a Jonathan Moore.

"No, I am Mexican—maybe you have guessed that? I have been in your country only short time. I do not know many people."

*Mexico!*

"Is your name, by any chance, Roberto Hermosa?" Joe asked.

The mechanic looked amused. "No. I never hear of Roberto Hermosa."

The Hardys' enthusiasm was waning but was not entirely dispelled. From a pocket Frank pulled a picture of the man they suspected of being Roberto Hermosa. "Have you ever seen this person?" he asked.

"No, I never see that man in my life. But you call him Hermosa. For several years I work at beautiful hacienda near Taxco. It called 'Vista Hermosa.' That mean 'Beautiful View!' You should visit."

Frank told the mechanic they were trying to locate the person shown in the picture.

"I wish I could help you," the Mexican replied.

"You really are a direct descendant of an Aztec warrior?" Joe asked. When the man nodded, the young sleuth added, "Just a few days ago we heard of someone else who makes the same claim." Joe did not mention Mr. Moore's will.

The Mexican gave a wide grin. "I have well-educated rival for my position as pure descendant. I have never seen him, but I know his name —Señor Tatloc."

"Where does he live?" Frank questioned quickly.

"I do not know. He travels around a lot digging."

"You mean he is an archaeologist?" Frank queried.

"That is right."

The Hardys asked several other questions, but the Mexican was unable to answer any of them. Finally they said good-by and went to the waiting room.

On his left arm was a tattoo of an Aztec warrior

"For Pete's sake, where have you fellows been?" said Chet. "I thought you'd flown off without me!"

"It would have served you right," Joe needled. "If you keep on eating, Chet, you'll be so overweight they won't take you on the plane."

"Oh, all right, all right," said Chet. "Now tell me what you've been doing." He was astounded upon learning that his friends had picked up a good clue.

"Señor Tatloc, eh?" he repeated. Then he gave a great sigh. "I can just see you fellows making me climb all over those crumbly old ruins!"

The boys' plane finally took off. After a delicious meal on board, they fell asleep. It was Sunday morning when they awoke, and the stewardess announced that they would land at the Mexico City airport in twenty minutes. The boys quickly washed, combed their hair, and straightened their rumpled suits. Then they watched from the windows as the great plane circled and came to a landing.

"Let's take a taxi into town," Frank suggested. "We'll get the driver to show us some of the interesting sights as we go along."

They found a taxi driver, who grinned in delight when he found the boys spoke his native tongue. He said he would be honored to take his passengers on a sightseeing trip before delivering them to their hotel.

The boys climbed into the car, and the driver sped out of the airport and onto a wide highway. The road was bordered by low stucco houses and open-air markets with here and there a tall apartment house.

"This doesn't look very old," Chet remarked. He sounded disappointed.

"Wait!" the driver advised. "We come to old part of city soon."

A short time later he turned into a large square. "This is the *zócalo*," he announced proudly. "The cathedral on the north side was finished in 1667 and built on the ruins of a great Aztec temple."

The boys gazed at the huge church with interest. Then, pointing to a long low building which covered one side of the plaza, the driver explained that this was the National Palace. On the other sides of the square were the Palacio Municipal and an arcade which sheltered a row of small shops.

"This part looks pretty old," Chet acknowledged.

Suddenly a taxi passed the one in which the boys were riding. A man's hand protruded from it. He was waving a white handkerchief frantically as if to attract their attention.

"Is that a signal to us?" Frank asked excitedly.

# CHAPTER VI

## Unwanted Passenger

"DRIVER, pull up alongside that taxi," Frank cried, pointing ahead.

The taximan put on a burst of speed, while the Hardys strained their eyes to see who was inside the other taxi.

They were barely able to catch a glimpse of its passengers, but Frank whispered, "That man with the handkerchief is Jack Wayne! The other man looks Mexican."

Suddenly their own taxi stopped. Quickly Frank and Joe turned to see why. To their amazement a stranger, with flashing black eyes and swarthy skin, and holding some kind of badge in his hand, was climbing in beside their driver.

"You're under arrest!" he told the taximan.

"What! I have done nothing!" the frightened driver said.

Frank and Joe looked at each other and at

Chet, who gulped nervously. Did this have something to do with them? Was this a ruse to capture them as well as Wayne? Frank whispered to the others, "We'd better get out of here—and fast!"

Joe nodded, grabbed his suitcase, and opened the door. The next moment he and Chet, swinging his bag, were on the street. Frank threw a bill to the taxi driver and hopped out with his luggage. The stranger ordered the taximan to hurry on.

Instantly horns began to toot at the boys, and cars swerved to avoid hitting them. Chet and the Hardys realized they were raising a traffic commotion. It was impossible for them to reach the sidewalk.

"I wanted to follow that other taxi," said Frank, as a car nearly sideswiped him.

"N-not me," quavered Chet. "We might be in jail by now!"

"We'll never be able to catch up with it now," said Joe as the brakes of a taxi near him screeched.

Finally the boys held up their hands and the motorists realized the trio's predicament. One car after another came to a grinding halt to let the visitors run to the sidewalk.

Chet, speechless with relief, sat down on his suitcase and wiped the perspiration from his face. "Don't ever do that to me again!" he pleaded. "I lost five years off my life."

"Too bad it wasn't ten pounds," said Joe. "We

took our lives in our hands—and all for nothing!"

Frank said it was his fault and asked if either of the boys had obtained the license number of the taxi carrying Jack Wayne. Neither of them had.

"I was too busy watching traffic," Joe confessed. "I did notice one thing, though. The taxi was yellow."

"And needed paint," Chet added.

"I saw a triangular dent in the right-hand back door," Frank said. "Well, that's pretty good identification. I think we should track down that taxi and quiz the driver."

"Not me!" Chet said firmly. "Do you realize all that has happened to us in the short time we've been in this city? I think you fellows imagined that was Jack Wayne. He would have called out to us. I vote we go to our hotel. Me for a bath and a nap."

Frank had spotted an empty taxi and hailed it. The boys climbed in with their luggage, and the driver was directed to their hotel. The room assigned to them was large and had three beds in it. Chet gave a flying leap and sprawled onto one of them.

"Boy, does this feel good!" He closed his eyes, and a minute later it was evident from his deep breathing that the stout boy was asleep.

"First casualty," Frank said with a grin. "I guess we'll have to carry on alone for a while."

He became serious. "It seems to me that Jack Wayne must still be a prisoner and was waving a distress signal."

"Do you suppose it was just a coincidence that he saw us?" Joe asked.

"I doubt it," Frank replied. "But I'm fairly sure that we weren't supposed to see him. His taxi was following us and because of the flow of traffic was forced to pass us. I'll bet the man who jumped into our taxi to arrest the driver was a phony and an accomplice of the abductors. Maybe it was an attempt to capture us."

"Good logic, but we still haven't a clue to who our enemies are," said Joe. "One thing seems certain. That Aztec warrior object must be mighty valuable."

Frank looked at Chet, then said, "Joe, while he's asleep, how about you and me going to police headquarters and reporting everything?"

"We certainly need all the help we can get," said Joe. "Let's go!"

Frank wrote a note to Chet, then the boys went downstairs and asked the way to the *policia*. It was not far, so the brothers decided to walk. When Chief Diaz heard their story he told them that the taxi driver had reported the incident of the attempted arrest. The phony officer had jumped out of the taxi at the next traffic light.

Gravely the chief said, "I had a report from the States about your friend Jack Wayne, but we have no leads to him. He did not land at our airport. Now you say he probably is in our city. I will use every method to find this man."

"We'd appreciate that," Frank said. "Perhaps you can also help us find two other men we are looking for—Señor Tatloc, the archaeologist, and a Roberto Hermosa." The chief promised he would help them in any way he could.

The boys thanked him and left. As they retraced their steps to the hotel, Joe said, "Why don't we hire a taxi and cruise around to see if we can find the one which was carrying Jack?"

Frank waved down an oncoming taxi. After the boys had jumped in, he described to the driver in Spanish the kind of car for which they were searching.

The man looked inquisitive. He said politely, "It is not for a driver like me, Gomez, to be curious about my passengers' wishes, but may I know why the two young gentlemen wish to locate this vehicle?"

Joe smiled. "Would you believe me if I told you we're after a kidnapper?"

The Mexican's black eyes blinked several times. "I do not wish to have any trouble with a kidnapper," he said, "but I will ride around the streets so you can find the car you seek."

He went up one street and down another, through alleyways and back onto the famous Paseo de la Reforma. There had been no sign of the yellow taxicab with a dent in a back door.

Gomez looked at his meter. "This ride will be very expensive for you," he said.

"Give us another ten minutes please," Frank replied, glancing at his watch. "That'll make it an even hour."

The time was just about up when suddenly Joe cried out, "I see it! Gomez, stop!"

Their driver pulled to the curb directly behind the yellow taxi. The boys asked Gomez to wait for them, then ran up to talk to the other driver.

"Excuse me," said Frank, "but we're trying to find a friend of ours—an American—and a Mexican companion. They were riding in your taxi a little over an hour ago. Do you know where they went?"

"*Sí, sí,*" the taximan replied. "I dropped them at the Lagunilla Market."

"Lagunilla Market?" Frank repeated. "What's that?"

The driver laughed. "It is a place where people go to find bargains. Most of the merchandise is old and poor. Once in a while, however, something fine turns up. The merchants there have bought most of their things from strangers, and occasionally it is stolen property."

"Let's have this man take us to the Lagunilla Market," Frank suggested. "I'll pay Gomez."

The boys changed taxis and were taken to an

old, shabby-looking section of town. The open-air market ran from one street to another. Many of the vendors had their merchandise spread out on straw mats or blankets on the ground. A few had small booths with canopies set up. They were loudly hawking their wares in both Spanish and English.

The Hardys soon found that the merchants were suspicious and the boys had to buy trinkets in order to get responses to their questions.

"We may go bankrupt before we get a clue," said Joe with a grin.

They had gone nearly the full length of the market when they came to a woman merchant selling silver jewelry. Frank put his question to her, and instead of being ignored, it was answered at once.

"I remember the men you speak of," she said with a smile, straightening the many-colored apron she wore. "The man from your country bought a handsome bracelet from me—a man's bracelet. It was studded with turquoise—a great bargain."

The young sleuths were grateful for the information. To show their appreciation they bought two bracelets that looked old enough to have been worn by Aztec women. Their mother and Aunt Gertrude, they decided, would be pleased to receive them as souvenir gifts.

Suddenly the Mexican woman's face clouded.

"The American was a very nice man, but I did not like his companion. He had a wicked face and I saw him buy a large knife."

The Hardys were startled and asked for further identification. She said he was short and rather stout. The brothers again thanked the woman. Feeling that they now had a clue for the police, they started back to their taxi.

Suddenly the woman called out, "When you find your friend, I hope you will not laugh at him. He put the bracelet on his arm and said he was going to wear it all the time."

The Hardys figured that Jack was using the bracelet as identification in case the Hardys should pick up his trail.

"Did you notice which way the men went from here?" Joe asked.

"No. I'm sorry."

The taximan drove them to headquarters where they dismissed him. Chief Diaz was surprised to see his visitors so soon again and commended them on their sleuthing ability.

"That turquoise bracelet is a fine clue," he said.

The boys returned to their hotel. To their surprise Chet was not in the room, but propped against the mirror of the bureau was a note:

"Mystery solved. Have gone to get the Aztec warrior. Will bring him to our room."

# CHAPTER VII

# *Mexican Disguise*

"IF Chet Morton can prove to me that he has found the Aztec warrior," said Joe, pacing the floor of his hotel room, "I'll give him a big fat five-dollar bill!"

Frank was staring out the window. "It would be worth a lot more. I just can't believe it!"

The brothers speculated excitedly about their pal's discovery. They did not dare leave the room for fear Chet might return, and they most certainly wanted to be on hand if the mystery had been solved!

Nearly an hour went by when a soft tap came on the door. Both brothers ran to open it. As they swung the door wide, Frank and Joe stared in disbelief.

*Standing before them was a plump figure in full Aztec warrior garb—feathered helmet, a long, elaborately embroidered tunic, and sandals!*

The figure strode into the room. As the light from the window fell on him, Frank and Joe's amazement turned to hilarity. They burst into guffaws of laughter, spun in half circles, and dropped onto the bed.

"Chet Morton, you loon!" Frank exclaimed. "Where did you get that outfit?"

"I guess we deserve having a joke played on us." Joe chuckled.

Chet Morton did not even smile. He stood looking at his chums with a hurt expression on his face. "This isn't funny," he said. "I figured the best way to get a lead on the living Aztec warrior was to wear this costume in the street and attract attention. Everybody will be asking questions and then we can ask some in return."

"You're likely to be taken to the funny farm," said Joe.

Slowly Chet removed the helmet. As he laid it on the bureau, he said, "I guess you fellows don't like my idea, and I thought it was such a good one. You don't know what a hard time I had finding a costume store that was open and carried this getup. And I paid a whole week's rental on it!" he added woefully.

"That's too bad," said Frank, grinning. "Maybe you ought to buy the costume and take it home. It sure would make a hit in Bayport."

"Okay. I will."

The stout boy was saved from further needling by the ringing of the telephone. Frank answered and learned that the call was from police headquarters. "Can you come right down?" Chief Diaz asked. "Your friend Jack Wayne is here."

"Really!" Frank exclaimed. "That's great. We'll be there pronto."

When he reported the news to the other boys, they were astounded. Joe remarked, "Mighty efficient police force, I'd say!"

The Hardys helped Chet out of his costume, then the trio raced downstairs to the hotel entrance. Frank flagged a taxi and soon they were hurrying into police headquarters.

"Jack!" the Hardys cried out joyfully upon seeing the pilot.

There were hearty handshakes, then Frank and Joe asked for the full story of the kidnapping and release.

Their lean, tanned friend looked haggard but produced a broad grin. Pointing to the silver-and-turquoise bracelet on his arm, he said, "This did it. If you fellows hadn't uncovered the clue, I might still be the prisoner of those lowdown weasels! The police quizzed people who saw me wearing it and trailed me to the house where I was tied up.

"Nobody else was there and those crooks haven't been captured yet. The only one whose face I ever saw was the man who climbed into your father's plane at the Bayport airfield, poked a gun into my ribs, and ordered me to take off. I didn't have any choice, but I was sure you Hardys would trail us."

As Jack Wayne paused, Frank said, "It's a lucky thing we saw your handkerchief signal this morning."

"Yes. My abductors threatened to harm me if I tried to escape, so I used that method to warn you that you were being followed."

While the chief took a phone call, the pilot added in a whisper, "The gang is after the Aztec warrior object, and my kidnapper tried to find out from me where it is. He said it's worth a fortune."

When the chief finished his call, Jack went on, "The kidnapper—I never did learn his name—directed me to land on a field at an abandoned farm outside this city. A group of masked men met us and put me in a car. Then we came into the city, and I was forced into a house. There I was made to answer a lot of questions about you Hardys. I probably shouldn't have bragged that I knew you would come after me.

"Then, the hijacker took me out to a taxi, and we drove to the big airport to watch you come in. We kept you in sight to find out where you were going. Suddenly the traffic forced us to pass your taxi. I decided to try that handkerchief signal to alert you."

"It did," said Joe. "And that man with a badge

who jumped into our taxi—we thought at first he was a detective—probably intended to kidnap us too."

"I know about him," said Jack. "He's one of the gang. He was in another taxi. As soon as he saw my warning signal to you, he got out of his taxi and stopped your driver. I was looking back and sure was glad when I saw you fellows hop out."

"Why were you taken to the Lagunilla Market?" Joe asked.

"So you wouldn't be able to pick up our trail and find out where I was being held," the pilot replied. "The men thought you'd probably quiz our driver, so we changed taxis at the Lagunilla Market. While we were there, the kidnapper purchased one of the wickedest-looking knives I've ever seen.

"I managed to persuade him to let me buy the bracelet. I wore it, hoping you fellows could trace me." Jack gave a broad grin. "And you did, thank goodness!"

Chet, who had been silent up to this time, reminded the pilot that he had said he knew only his kidnapper. "Would you recognize the man who got in our taxi if you saw him again?"

"I couldn't see his face," said Jack. "By the way, the hijacker told me he had tried to break into Mr. Moore's home, but that you'd stopped him."

"We didn't get a very good look at him," said Frank. "He's short and dark. What else can you tell us about him?"

"The outstanding thing about him is that his teeth are quite crooked and overlapping."

The Hardys and Chet further learned that a man referred to as Jimenez seemed to be the leader of the group.

Chief Diaz spoke up. "He and his friends may be hard to capture. I feel sure none of them will return to the house where we found you, Señor Wayne. The gang probably had a lookout, and when we tracked you down, he no doubt warned those scoundrels and they got away in a hurry."

The officer promised that his department would continue their search. In the meantime, if the pilot was ready, they would drive him to his plane, which the police had learned was still where it had been landed. "I understand you wish to get back to Bayport as soon as possible."

"That's right," Jack replied.

While the chief was making arrangements, the pilot whispered to the boys, "I'm sorry I couldn't find out more about the Aztec warrior—both the thing and the man."

Frank spoke up, "Jack, you've done a great job and given us some important clues. It's too bad you had to be kidnapped in the process, but it sure is paying off."

After Jack had left in the police car, the boys

talked over what their next move should be. They decided to go at once to the University of Mexico and try to talk to someone connected with the archaeological department about Señor Tatloc. Since the buildings were some distance out of town, they took a taxi.

Along the way were beautiful new homes, most of them a delicate shade of pink concrete. All were set among rolling lawns and gardens of profuse, bright-colored flowers.

As the taxi drew near the university buildings, Chet leaned out the window and gaped in amazement. "Boy, look at that!" he exclaimed, gazing at the beautiful, intricate mosaic work which formed the walls of the huge library.

One side showed a gigantic figure—half of it representing the Indian background of Mexico, the other its Spanish influence.

At the administration building Frank asked the driver to stop while he went inside to inquire if he could see a staff member of the archaeological department. He was given directions to the nearby home of Professor Rincon. The boys found it and requested the taxi driver to wait for them.

Professor Rincon was a friendly, scholarly person who said he knew Señor Maxli Tatloc well, and identified him as one of the two men in the photographic prints. "I have not seen him in a long time, however. Tatloc is a very retiring person and moves often. I believe he has no permanent residence.

"Tatloc is greatly sought after but hard to find. He spends practically all his time at various ruins and has dug up some very interesting relics. It is strange, but he never bothers to deliver these himself either to government or private museums. He always sends them by messengers."

Frank said the boys were eager to locate Tatloc. "But evidently we'll have a hard time doing it," he said, smiling.

"I'm afraid so," said the professor, "because there are not only the well-known ruins but also many still to be unearthed."

"Thank you very much," said Joe. "I guess we'd better get started on our hunt."

Professor Rincon wished the boys luck. "If you find Señor Tatloc, please give him my best regards and tell him I should like him to speak before some of my classes."

The three boys went back to their waiting taxi. Frank looked at his wristwatch. "Too late to see any ruins today," he remarked with a sigh, "but tomorrow let's hire a car and go to the closest ruin, Teotihuacan."

"Isn't that the place where Mr. Moore took a picture of his friend in costume?" Chet asked.

"Yes."

The Hardys and Chet spent the evening studying the various pictures they had brought and a list of all ruins which were accessible by car.

"If we don't have any luck, we'll try the less accessible ones later," Joe said.

Chet was particularly interested in the Teotihuacan ruins, originally the religious center of the Toltecs and later invaded by the Aztecs.

"This Pyramid of the Sun sure looks high," he remarked. "You fellows aren't going to make me climb to the top of that to hunt for a clue to Señor Tatloc, are you?"

The Hardys grinned, and Joe said, "I promise it'll take a few pounds off you. But then, I'm not sure you could get to the top without puffing to death."

"Listen, I have more extra wind in my lungs than anybody on the Bayport High football team," Chet declared.

"You're absolutely right," said Frank. "And that's why you're elected to climb to the top first and tell us if there's anything worth going up there to look at!"

Chet retaliated by picking up a pillow and heaving it at Frank's head.

"So you want to get in practice, eh?" Joe asked. "Okay, here goes!"

For a few minutes pillows flew back and forth until Frank advised the boys to quit before the pillows burst and spread their contents all over the room. Shortly afterward, they went to bed.

Directly after breakfast Monday morning the

three chums went to an automobile rental agency. They chose a convertible and headed for Teotihuacan.

As it neared noontime, Chet smiled and smacked his lips. "Let's stop at the Grotto restaurant," he suggested.

Frank turned off the road and went to the famous restaurant in a mammoth cave. The Bayporters found it to be a unique eating place, and thought of the time when some ancient Indian tribe had lived there.

Chet was about to order a second tamale when Frank cautioned him, "Remember, we have a long climb ahead." Reluctantly, Chet changed his mind.

When the boys' car reached the area of the great four-sided pyramids with their hundreds of shallow steps, the three young visitors stared in wonder. The area was teeming with groups of diggers in various phases of uncovering further buried ruins.

"Wow!" Joe exclaimed. "We expected to find a ghost city—and instead it's crowded with archaeologists."

Chet looked up at the Pyramid of the Sun in awe. "Boy, this is a lot higher when you're nearby—it almost reaches the sun! And just to let you know I'm no sissy, I'm going partway to the top."

As he started straight up the narrow steps, Joe called out after him, "Hey! Remember the ancient Indians said you should put your feet sideways on the steps and zigzag when you go up or down."

Frank and Joe started up in this fashion, but Chet paid no attention to their advice. He had climbed about thirty feet when suddenly one foot slipped. Down he went, clutching wildly at the craggy steps but unable to get a hold. Now he began to roll over and over toward the bottom.

Joe was some distance away and too far down to help his chum. Frank, closer at hand, tried to stop Chet's rapid descent. But the tumbling figure knocked him over and the two boys spun down helter-skelter, gathering speed as they went!

# CHAPTER VIII

## *Ambushed Detectives*

BRUISED and scraped, Frank and Chet picked themselves up from the foot of the great pyramid. Joe hurried down the steps to see if the boys were all right.

He was relieved to find they were only dirty and shaken up. "You fellows looked like something out of an old-time comedy routine," he said, chuckling.

Chet eyed Joe for a moment, then remarked, "I feel as if I'd been rolling for the past thousand years!"

Frank heaved a long sigh. "Well, I'm ready to try it again. You guys all set?"

It took Chet nearly half a minute to decide that he would accompany the Hardys. This time, the boys made the ascent more slowly and finally reached the flat summit. They walked all around it, gazing down in every direction.

"Boy, what a city this must have been!" Joe said. "All these temples kept people busy building, repairing, and preparing for the human sacrifices."

"I read that a hundred thousand people lived here," Chet spoke up. He pointed off some distance. "That's the Pyramid of the Moon, isn't it?" The Hardys nodded.

The pyramid was similar to the one on which they stood, except it was considerably smaller.

Frank indicated a temple. "That's the one built in honor of a foreigner."

"What!" Chet cried. "I thought it was erected a thousand years before the Spaniards came here."

"It was. Haven't you heard the legend? It seems a man of fair skin, long beard, and blue eyes arrived from across the ocean—some people say he was riding a plumed serpent and that is why the serpent was sacred to Mexicans in ancient times. This man, whom they called Quetzalcoatl—quetzal for their venerated bird—had knowledge far superior to that of the Indians who were here. He taught them how to build, raise food, and become skilled in the art of stone carving."

"Did he live with the Aztecs?" Chet asked.

"No. He was here long before they came. After his death, the natives made Quetzalcoatl one of their gods."

The three boys started zigzagging down the steps of the pyramid. Halfway to the bottom, Joe called out, "Fellows, see that man down there? He looks like the one in our pictures!"

"Señor Tatloc?" Chet queried.

"Could be." Joe nodded as he put on more speed.

By the time he reached the base of the pyramid, the man was nowhere in sight. Thinking he had gone to another side of the pyramid, the trio sprinted along the base until they came to a corner, and turned down the side. Still the stranger was not to be seen.

The Hardys and Chet circled the base of the tremendous structure, but he had vanished.

Chet dropped to the ground, exhausted. "I just knew I was letting myself in for something," he panted. "It would have been much easier walking around Mexico City in my Aztec costume."

Frank and Joe did not answer. They were pretty winded themselves. Finally Joe remarked, "Those old Aztecs sure had lung power."

Frank suggested that perhaps the stranger they sought had gone to another pyramid. The boys went to their car and drove first to the Pyramid of the Moon. The man was not there, so they set off for the Temple of Quetzalcoatl.

They went completely around the pyramid, scanning the steps and the ground for a glimpse of the elusive man.

Frank frowned. "That probably *was* Señor Tatloc. Since he's such a retiring person he would have hurried away when he saw us."

"That's just great," said Chet. "If he takes off every time we spot him, how are we ever going to talk to him?" The stout boy sighed. "Oh, well, maybe the guy we saw wasn't Tatloc, anyway."

The boys spent the next hour examining the weird carvings on the temple. There were huge heads of serpents with open jaws and wicked-looking teeth. Interspersed among the stone reptiles were heads, which they figured represented the god Quetzalcoatl.

"He has on a flat top hat," said Chet with a grin, and added, "That must have been the style during the period he was a human—not so fancy as the ones the Aztecs wore later."

The three visitors marveled at the number of carvings which stretched not only along the base of the pyramid but in rows up the sides.

"Do you suppose," said Frank, "that Mr. Moore's slides indicate we'll find a clue here to the Aztec warrior object? This is certainly the place where he took one picture."

Joe surveyed the huge temple. "If you mean some letter or document is hidden in one of these carvings, it would take us at least a month to search for them."

The Hardys decided that they could always come back to the Temple of Quetzalcoatl. In the meantime, they would search at various other ruins to find Señor Tatloc.

The boys drove away. As they neared the outskirts of Mexico City, Chet proposed that they eat at a real Mexican restaurant. He directed the way to a long narrow building. Frank found a parking place some distance down the street.

The restaurant had booths for four on each side of a wide aisle. A man in a black velvet, gold-embroidered, tight-fitting suit and a large black hat which he wore at a rakish angle was playing a guitar at the rear of the restaurant. Couples were dancing in the aisles.

The three boys were shown to a booth. After looking over the menu they ordered bean soup, roast chicken without the chocolate pepper sauce, and totopos—an American-type frito served with a sauce made of mashed avocado, boiled tomato, olive oil, onion, salt, and lemon.

"Mm, this hits me just right," said Chet, after sampling all the dishes.

At that moment the music stopped. The hungry boys ate rather than talked and could plainly hear the chatter around them. Suddenly the Hardys detected a voice in the booth behind them asking the waiter in Spanish to find out the boys' destination. It occurred to the Hardys that the man might belong to the kidnapping gang!

Frank, who had the aisle seat, leaned out and looked around. Four men occupied the booth.

One, young with an evil-looking face, was handing the waiter a tip. Instantly Frank drew back and put a finger to his lips as a sign for Joe and Chet to let him do the talking.

When the waiter reached the boys' booth, he asked Frank in Spanish where the boys were going.

"I don't understand," Frank said vaguely.

By signs and gestures the waiter tried his best to get the message across. At last he shrugged, gave up, and went back to the other booth. He reported that the boys did not speak Spanish.

The three chums grinned and tried to hear the conversation of the inquirer and his friends. But the men had dropped their voices to whispers.

In turn Frank lowered his, saying, "Maybe these men aren't part of the gang, but just plain thugs out to rob us. If they follow us from the restaurant, we can be sure they're up to no good."

"What'll we do?" Chet quavered.

"How about giving them the old football rush?" Joe suggested.

To the Hardys' surprise, the episode took away Chet's appetite. He not only did not finish the food in front of him, but refused dessert.

"Players shouldn't eat much before a game, anyhow," Joe remarked. "Let's go!"

The three boys had barely reached the sidewalk when the four men from the booth started after them. Chet and the Hardys walked fast, thinking that if they could reach the car, then they could make it safely to the hotel.

The men behind them apparently anticipated the boys' plan and decided to act in a hurry. As the young sleuths reached an alleyway, the four men converged on them. Instantly the Americans were forced into the dark alley!

## CHAPTER IX

## *Iguana Scare*

To THE surprise of the Mexicans, the Hardys and Chet instantly turned around and rushed at them like battering rams. Chet knocked out one man, and he fell to the cobblestone pavement.

The Hardys' fists flew and their arms flailed with telling blows. The other three Mexicans were so thunderstruck that within seconds they gave up the fight and fled down the dark alley.

Joe started after them, but Frank grabbed his brother's arm. "We don't know what's down there. The men may have reinforcements."

Joe paused. "Anyway, we have one captive for the police."

By this time a small crowd had gathered, and an officer pushed his way through. Frank explained what had happened.

The man on the ground, who was beginning to regain consciousness, was dragged by his arms out to the sidewalk. In the street light the policeman recognized him.

"This man is a wanted local hoodlum," the officer said. "He and his friends prey on tourists." Looking at the Hardys and Chet, the policeman added, "You boys certainly defended yourselves well." He smiled. "You are athletic— maybe you should train to become matadors!"

The three boys laughed and Chet said, "No thank you. I'll stick to football. I don't want to ram into anything with horns."

The dejected hoodlum, still in a somewhat groggy state, was marched to a police sedan. Frank, Joe, and Chet were requested to go along in their own car and tell their story to the officer in charge.

When the boys arrived at headquarters, Chief Diaz was there. He was not on duty but had dropped in to pick up some papers. When he heard the story of the encounter, the officer beamed at them.

"Bravo!" he said. "We could use more of your kind here to help us discipline our lawbreakers."

Chief Diaz waited until the boys had made a formal charge against their attackers, then he walked outside with them.

"I have been trying to reach you boys on the phone to tell you something," he said. "A few hours ago I heard a rumor that an archaeologist had just made a great discovery at Monte Alban. I wondered if he might be the man you're looking for."

"Señor Tatloc?" Frank asked.

"No one knows," the officer answered. "The report was that a traveler had arrived in town with the information. He said the archaeologist did not wish to be identified. I'm inclined to think he may be Señor Tatloc."

"Then we shouldn't waste any time getting down to those ruins and looking for him," Joe said eagerly.

The Hardys queried the chief further about what the discovery was. His information was scanty. The traveler who had reported the news had not revealed the nature of the find.

The archaeologist probably was still at Monte Alban, looking for other treasures of antiquity. If he were Señor Tatloc, the boys had a good chance of locating him!

"It's pretty late to start for the ruins tonight," Frank remarked. "I hear there's a long detour through the mountains. Suppose we get up early tomorrow. With steady driving we should be there by evening."

When the boys reached their hotel room, they studied the map and decided to stop at Oaxaca, a small city three hundred and fifty miles southeast of Mexico City.

"We'll stay at a hotel there," Frank said, "then go out to Monte Alban."

The young detectives got an early start but found plenty of traffic on the Pan-American Highway. In a couple of hours they had to branch off onto secondary roads through the mountains. There were sharp curves which Frank took carefully, sounding his horn frequently. Approaching drivers, apparently familiar with the road, did not bother to warn of their approach and whizzed around the corners at breakneck speed.

"Whew!" cried Chet, as a car narrowly missed them. "That driver must have hot tamales in his engine!"

The boys found the scenery gorgeous. Mountains were rugged, steep, and often merely bare granite rock. Some were gray in color, reminding the boys of those they were used to seeing in the Bayport area. But a great many cliffs were pink and in the dazzling sunlight stood out like rare paintings.

Joe was particularly impressed with the cacti. There were many varieties—from the low-growing, tulip-shaped maguey to the mammoth candle cactus. This resembled a giant green-and-silver candelabra with very tall candles of the same color.

Once the travelers came to a plateau on which grew a cactus orchard.

"Hey! Wait a minute!" Chet cried out.

Frank pulled to the side of the road and stopped. Chet pointed to a Mexican, wearing an enormous sombrero, who was kneeling on the ground, his face buried in one of the cactus plants.

"I guess he's having a drink," said Joe. "Shall we all go over and get one?"

"I'm not sure we should drink raw cactus juice," Frank said, "but let's talk to the man anyway."

As the boys drew closer, they were astounded to see what the Mexican was doing. As he raised his head from the plant, he held a long brown thorn in his teeth. To it was attached what looked like a stout white thread. To the boys' amazement, the man kept tugging like a bird pulling a worm from the soil. In a few moments he stood up with a thread a yard long dangling from the thorn, which the boys now could see was as sharp on the end as a needle.

"*Buenos dias,*" said Frank. He continued in Spanish, "We are curious to know what you intend to do with this."

The Mexican grinned. "My good wife will mend my clothes with it," he said. "Cactus thread is very strong." The man demonstrated by pushing the cactus needle through his shirt as if he were sewing. "Would you like to take this with you for a souvenir?" he asked.

"*Gracias,*" said Frank. "We may need it!"

"You know about the cactus plant?" the man asked. "Every part of it is used—from the leaves we make thatched roofs for our huts and fibers

to weave cloth. In the desert many weary travelers have stayed alive by drinking cactus juice."

Hearing this, Chet decided to try a drink. He
asked how he could suck the liquid out of the
plant. The man laughed and said this would be
hard for anyone as stout as Chet.

The Hardys smothered grins, but their pal
took the remark good-naturedly. The Mexican
then offered to get a siphon. He hurried off to a
thatched roof hut nearby and soon returned with
the equipment. The man chose one of the older
plants, saying the juice from it would be more
palatable, and inserted a narrow hose down inside it. He told Chet to put the other end of the
hose into his mouth and suck.

Chet went about this eagerly. It took several
seconds, and he was red in the face before the
sap of the plant began to come out. After two
mouthfuls, Chet took the hose from his mouth.

"You like it?" the Mexican asked.

Chet did not, but he wanted to be polite. "It's
a little too sticky for me," he replied.

Before leaving, Frank and Joe each took a couple of mouthfuls. They agreed with Chet that
this was all they wanted to drink of the sweet
liquid. They thanked the native for his kindness
and drove on.

It was not long before Chet gave a great yawn
and announced that he was ready for the lunch
which the hotel had packed, then for a rest. They

chose a pleasant little patch of woods near a stream.

"I hope this box has something good in it," the stout boy remarked, untying the string.

Inside he found cheese sandwiches, hard-boiled eggs, a quantity of cookies, and several oranges.

"Not a thing Mexican," he said in some disappointment.

"Anyway. you started with maguey juice," Joe reminded him.

When the boys finished eating, the Hardys were eager to be on their way. Chet rebelled. "What's the hurry?" he asked, yawning. "I sure need a nap. 1 won't sleep long, fellows, honest."

Chet propped himself against a tree and in a few moments was fast asleep. Frank and Joe

walked around for exercise. On their return they noticed a barefoot Mexican boy approaching them. As the Hardys came nearer, he stopped and smiled in a friendly way. When Frank and Joe spoke to the lad in Spanish, he was delighted.

"You are North Americans," he said. "I learn in school that you have a great country. You shoot off rockets toward the moon. I would like to go to the moon someday."

The Hardys grinned. "You probably will," Frank predicted.

The native youngster was extremely intelligent, and although his clothes indicated that he lived on a farm which was not too prosperous, his face showed eagerness and willingness to learn.

Suddenly the Mexican boy's expression changed to one of alarm as he looked beyond the Hardys. The next moment he made a dive past them.

Frank and Joe turned just in time to see a large iguana moving swiftly toward the sleeping Chet.

The little boy by this time had reached Chet's side. Sweeping his right arm downward, he grabbed the iguana by the back of the neck and the tail, and yanked it up into the air. He cried out something in an Indian tongue to the reptile, which wriggled to free itself. But all it could do was claw the air and hiss.

The commotion awakened Chet, who stared in disbelief. For a moment he thought the boy was going to throw the iguana on him and dashed out of the way.

"Where'd that ugly thing come from?" he exclaimed. "Take it away!"

By now, the Mexican boy was smiling again. He explained that the iguana must have crawled for some distance from a valley near a river.

"I thought iguanas were harmless," said Frank.

"They are," the lad answered. "But I was

afraid that if your friend woke up and saw it, it might give him a bad scare."

Chet thanked the boy profusely, and before starting off with the Hardys, he handed his "rescuer" several coins.

"See you on the moon someday!" Joe called out as their car pulled away.

It was late afternoon when the three boys reached Oaxaca. They decided to stay at a hotel on the edge of town. After registering and unloading their baggage, the three set off for a look at the town.

They had not gone far when Frank called, "Listen!"

He and the others stopped. From a distance ahead of them came sounds of music and shouting. The boys could not tell from the babble of voices whether they were sounds of merriment or of some kind of protest meeting.

"How about our finding out what's going on?" Frank suggested.

## CHAPTER X

## *Ghost-City Search*

FRANK, Joe, and Chet soon found that the shouting they heard came from the *zócalo*. The large square was being used as a stage, with an enthusiastic audience standing around its sides.

"No trouble here," said Joe in relief. "Just a celebration."

They watched a group of children in gay Spanish costumes dancing to the music of several guitars. Chet and the Hardys observed with interest the intricate steps such small boys and girls could accomplish.

A bystander heard Frank's admiring comments and said, "Children in Mexican schools have regular instruction in native dances at an early age. Many become professional dancers."

Frank asked whether schools taught only the Spanish-dominated period in the country's his-

tory. The man shook his head. "Our pupils learn
the history of Mexico from prehistoric times.
Many of them can speak the various Indian dia-
lects, and through legends handed down in their
families, know a lot about the great civilizations
that were here in ancient days."

The children's performance came to an end
and they ran off, giggling and bowing. The next
number on the program brought rapt attention,
not only from the native audience but from the
Bayport visitors.

A group of men were costumed as ancient warriors. Their act, done in dance form, represented
a battle. The soldiers used long-handled daggers
with which they fenced adroitly to overcome
their opponents.

"They're great!" said Chet.

"Sure are," the Hardys agreed.

Presently it became evident that one side was
victorious, when most of their opponents fell as
if slain. In rushed a man dressed as an ancient
priest, holding up his hand to end the slaughter.
He commanded the victors to bring him one of
the conquered warriors who was still on his feet
and ordered the man to follow him.

The priest cried out, "You have been chosen
for the human sacrifice!"

"Ugh!" said Chet. "That old fellow looks fierce
enough to carry out his threat!"

The Hardys and the friendly man who stood

next to them laughed, and the stranger said, "I am glad that you found the performance so realistic. You could almost believe there was to be a sacrifice. We Spanish stopped that ugly custom among the ancient people. It took many, many years to convince the Indians that their gods were not demanding this form of obeisance."

"All I can say," Chet spoke up, "is that I'm glad I'm living today. I would have been too nice a fat morsel for those bloodthirsty people!"

The man hastened to assure Chet that the Indians were not cannibals. They carried on human sacrifice only in accordance with their religion.

When the performance was over, Frank asked the Mexican if he knew anyone named Roberto Hermosa.

"No, I'm sorry. Does he live in Oaxaca?"

"We don't know," Frank replied. He pulled one of the photographs of Tatloc from his pocket. "This is another man we're trying to find. He is an archaeologist named Señor Tatloc. Have you ever heard of him?"

"*Sí, sí,*" the man answered quickly. "I have never seen him, but I have heard that a Señor Tatloc has dug many times in ruins near here."

"At Monte Alban?" Joe asked eagerly.

"That I do not know," their informer replied.

The boys thanked him and said good-by. Then they questioned some of the dancers and onlookers who stood around. None of them knew

Hermosa or Señor Tatloc nor did they recognize the photograph.

"We had a good time, but so far as the mystery is concerned, we drew a blank," said Frank with disappointment, as the boys trudged back to their hotel.

There they talked with the manager, but he could not help them either. He had not even heard the story of the prize relic having been found at Monte Alban.

Joe changed the subject and asked how early they might eat dinner. "Six o'clock," was the reply.

At once Joe proposed that the boys eat early and then drive out to the Monte Alban ruins to search for Tatloc. "It doesn't get dark until late. What say?"

The others agreed and by seven o'clock the three sleuths were on their way. Unfortunately, they were not familiar with the road and presently found themselves off course. To get back in the right direction, they took an unpaved and rather desolate side road.

Chet, who was riding in the back seat alone, began to complain. "My supper's going to be jounced down in twenty minutes at this rough rate," he said, almost hitting the top of the car as Frank drove in and out of deep ruts.

To Frank, the pace seemed very slow. "I hope this won't last long," he said worriedly.

"Good place for a blowout," Joe remarked.

"And a—a holdup!" Chet added.

Fortunately, the boys reached a paved road without any tire or engine trouble. Frank put on speed, and the car climbed the mountain to the ruins. The delay had been costly in terms of time, and when they reached the summit of Monte Alban, the sun had set and the moon had already come out.

"We mustn't forget our flashlights," Frank reminded the others. "And, Chet, look out for ghosts!"

The stout boy gave a grunt. "No ghost's going to come after me. He'll be looking for two guys named Hardy who are searching for an Aztec warrior."

"Okay, Chet, you win," Frank conceded.

In the moonlight the great pyramidal temples, tombs, and palaces of Monte Alban looked ghostly and weird indeed. The boys found a tremendous esplanade with giant structures surrounding it. Frank parked the car at one of the openings between the buildings, and the boys proceeded on foot. All of them felt a sense of awe at the immensity and silence of the area where once there had been so much activity.

"What's the history of this spot?" Chet asked, as he looked warily from left to right.

"I understand that during the early fifteen hundreds it was a city," said Frank, "but after the place was captured, the new owners built another city and used this one just to bury their great leaders and to hold religious ceremonials."

"Then it *is* a ghost city," said Chet. They were passing a stone wall on which were carved life-sized figures of dancers. "Wow!" Chet cried out, pushing against the Hardys. "Look!"

Frank and Joe turned. "What's up?"

"They're—they're alive!" Chet murmured.

The brothers began to laugh. "You're going loco!" said Joe. For fun he went up to the wall, pretended to put his arm around one of the figures, and performed a few dance steps.

Chet did not join the hilarity. "I *don't* care what you fellows say, I think there are haunts around here. It's too spooky for me. Let's go!"

"Not on your life!" said Frank. "Have you forgotten why we came? We're looking for Señor Tatloc."

"But you're not going to find him," Chet predicted. "Even if he does work on the ruins, why would he stay at night?"

Chet had almost convinced the Hardys he was right, when suddenly Joe cried softly, "Look!"

At the top of a pyramid just ahead was a flickering light, like that of a lantern.

"We're in luck!" Joe said excitedly. "That might be Señor Tatloc up there."

Frank looked doubtful. He suggested that the whole story of the archaeologist's being at the ruins might have been a hoax. He reminded his brother that the hotel manager had not heard of the great discovery.

"But why would anybody make up such a story?" Joe asked.

"It's a long guess, but it might even have been done to lure us out here," Frank answered. "Our enemies would know that we would be sure to investigate. We'll go up that pyramid and see what the light's all about. But we'd better be on our guard."

This latest thought of Frank's did not please Chet. He said he wished the three of them had never come and why didn't they go home at once?

The Hardys did not answer. They were already scrambling up the steps at a fast pace. Chet remained below, debating with himself what to do. He did not relish running into Wayne's kidnapper or the mysterious Mexican named Jimenez. On the other hand, he did not want to be left alone.

Frank and Joe, eager to get to the top, had not noticed that Chet had stayed behind. Suddenly their chum let out an agonizing yell.

"Look out, fellows! There are—"

At that moment something hit Chet hard on the head. He blacked out!

# CHAPTER XI

## *Yankee Warning*

HEARING Chet's warning, Frank and Joe turned abruptly. Two shadowy figures had sneaked up near them. Each held a raised club, about to descend on the Hardys' heads!

With quick reflexes, Frank and Joe struck out and sent their assailants spinning down the steps. Then the brothers raced for the top of the pyramid.

As they ran Frank gasped, "Maybe we're running into a trap! The light on top may belong to the gang that's after us!"

"You mean we'd better not take a chance?" Joe asked.

Frank continued to dash upwards, saying, "I don't think we have any choice. We know there are enemies below and—"

He suddenly stopped talking and stood still.

After gazing all around, he said worriedly, "Where's Chet?"

Joe looked about him. The moonlight was bright enough for him to get a clear view of the steps. Chet was not on them.

"I guess he didn't follow us," Joe said finally. "When Chet saw those men, he ran away."

"But where is he?" Frank persisted. "He may have been attacked!"

Their eyes roved slowly across the great plaza below them. There was no sign of their chum.

Panic seized the Hardys. "Those hoods we knocked down probably got him!" Frank gritted.

"But Chet warned us," Joe reminded his brother. "Why wouldn't he have run away?"

"The men who tried to club us probably had pals with them," Frank reasoned. "They nabbed Chet!"

The Hardys wasted no more time in conversation. Abandoning the plan to find out who had been using the light at the top of the pyramid, they hurried down to the base. Without depending entirely on moonlight for their search, the brothers swung their flashlights in great arcs. They failed to pick up any trace of their chum. Sure now that he had been kidnapped, the boys berated themselves for failing to check on him when they had started up the steps.

"How could we be so stupid?" Joe said glumly. "I suppose we'll have to go back to town and—"

He stopped speaking as the boys noticed two figures hurrying from a doorway in one of the ancient stone buildings. Instinctively, the Hardys followed. But the men were some distance ahead and apparently more familiar with the place than the brothers. They turned a corner of a temple and disappeared.

Frank and Joe doubled their speed but were unable to catch a glimpse of the fleeing figures. A few minutes later they heard the roar of a car motor and were sure that the men had left the area.

"One thing is certain," said Joe. "They didn't have Chet with them."

Frank nodded. "Which leads me to believe that they may have left him in that building they came out of."

The brothers started back on a run. When they reached the doorway, the boys beamed their lights inside. It revealed nothing but an empty room.

"Maybe Chet's tied up nearby," Joe suggested. "Let's call him."

He shouted into the building, then outdoors. There was no reply.

"We've heard only one car leave," said Frank. "If some of the gang took Chet with them, they carried him off before those two men fled. And if they did, we certainly aren't going to find him here."

Nevertheless, Joe continued to call his friend's name. Finally he stopped and the two boys stood still, trying to decide on their next move.

Frank suddenly shifted his weight. "I heard something!" he whispered.

The brothers listened intently. A sound like a muffled groan came to their ears.

"It must be inside this building," Frank insisted.

The brothers inspected the walls of the room. At one point there was a chest-high narrow opening, almost filled with several large loose stones. They were apparently part of an ancient doorway. Through it, the Hardys could hear the groaning more plainly. Working frantically, they began tearing down the blockade.

The Hardys squirmed through the opening, and Frank swung his flashlight around a small inner room. On the floor lay Chet Morton, semiconscious!

Frank and Joe leaped to examine their stout friend. Evidently he had been struck on the head, but otherwise he appeared to be uninjured.

"I wish I knew where there was some water," said Frank. "It might help revive him."

The sound of Frank's voice seemed to have a stimulating effect on Chet. He blinked his eyes open and looked uncertainly about him.

"Chet!" Frank and Joe cried out together, and Frank added, "Thank goodness you're all right!"

Chet was too groggy to talk. But being used to rugged treatment in football games, he tried to sit up.

"We'll take you outside into the fresh air," said Frank.

He and Joe carefully raised Chet to a standing position. Then, supporting him under his arms, they helped him out to the esplanade. He took several deep breaths of air and seemed to be somewhat refreshed.

"Did somebody hit you?" Frank asked.

"I—I guess so," Chet answered weakly. As his head cleared, he said, "I'm glad you fellows are all right. Boy, when I saw those two guys with the clubs about to hit you on the noggin, I nearly passed out. You heard me yell, didn't you?"

"We sure did," Joe told him. "Thanks for saving our necks."

Suddenly Chet began to wobble. The Hardys grabbed him and insisted that they go back to the hotel at once. Supporting him again, they made the trek to their car. For a moment Frank was worried that their unknown assailants might have tampered with the automobile. To his relief, as soon as he turned on the ignition, the motor roared to life.

As they started off, all three boys wondered what the mysterious assailants had hoped to accomplish. Were they part of the gang looking for the valuable Aztec warrior and still harassing the threesome to keep them from proceeding with their detective work?

"Whoever they were," said Chet, "you Hardys were too smart for them. I'm sorry I fouled you up and you couldn't find out about that light on top of the pyramid. Do you suppose those gangsters hide out up there?"

"I doubt it," said Frank. "It would be too noticeable. Maybe some of our questions can be answered if we come back tomorrow and search Monte Alban in the daylight."

Chet said nothing. His head ached, and he felt a little dizzy. "Bed sure will feel good," he said. He did not mention that he hoped Frank and Joe would make the trip by themselves the following day.

Actually the Hardys had the same idea. But they decided to wait until morning before saying anything to Chet.

When they reached their hotel room, the dazed boy dropped onto his bed. "I think I'll sleep with my clothes on," he said. "Too much trouble to take 'em off." His voice faded.

"We'll do it," the Hardys offered.

First, they removed his jacket and hung it up. Next came his shoes and socks, then his trousers.

As Frank unbuttoned Chet's sport shirt, a wadded piece of paper fell to the floor.

Frank picked it up. "What's this?" he asked.

Chet, who had closed his eyes, responded sleepily, "What's what?"

"This piece of paper you wadded up and put inside your shirt."

"I didn't put anything in my shirt," Chet insisted.

Eagerly Joe grabbed the paper and smoothed it out. Printed boldly in Spanish was a warning. Joe blinked, but refrained from reading it aloud, not wishing to disturb Chet any further.

Frank sensed that his brother had found something important but waited. The stout boy had become drowsy again and said nothing more about the paper. The Hardys finished undressing him and put on his pajamas. Within another thirty seconds, Chet was fast asleep.

Frank counted his friend's pulse beat. "He's okay, Joe."

Quickly moving to the bureau where Joe had laid the paper, Frank gasped in astonishment. The message read:

*Yankees go home. You cannot steal any of our treasures. If you disobey, you will lose your lives!*

# CHAPTER XII

# *"Five Rabbit"*

IN whispers, so they would not awaken Chet, Frank and Joe discussed the strange warning.

"I think we should take it to the local police," said Frank.

At the hotel desk Joe asked the manager if it would be safe for them to be on the streets alone at this hour of night. Mr. Perez looked at them in surprise and said that Oaxaca was a very fine town with excellent police protection.

"No offense intended," said Joe, "My brother and I were attacked recently in Mexico City."

"Oh, I understand now." Mr. Perez smiled. "You wish to go to a restaurant?"

"We may drop in for a midnight snack," said Joe, not wishing to give his real reason for going out. "If we get into any trouble, we'll make a beeline to police headquarters." He grinned. "Where is it, by the way?"

Mr. Perez gave them directions and the boys set off. At headquarters they told the officer on duty, Captain Valero, what had happened to Chet and themselves at the Monte Alban ruins.

The officer frowned. "I am sorry you were subjected to this indignity. Did you bring the paper with you?"

Frank handed it to Captain Valero, who read it several times. Finally he spoke up. "There's a band of young reactionaries in this area, I am sorry to say, and this may be more of their work. Their motives are perhaps laudable, but they should not try to act independently of the law."

Frank and Joe, puzzled, asked what the young men did.

Captain Valero replied, "They are against visitors from your country and from every other nation. They have an idea that sightseers come here for the sole purpose of stealing our relics. As you know, there is a law that anything of value found in Mexico must be turned over to our government. The presentation is often made to a museum." He smiled. "Our State Museum here in Oaxaca has a priceless collection of artifacts. You must visit it."

"But it isn't true that all visitors from the United States come here with theft in mind," Joe protested.

"The authorities know that," the captain stated, "but it is difficult to persuade hotheaded young men that they are wrong in the methods they use to carry out their fanaticism."

Frank changed the subject. "Joe and I are down here looking for two men. That is why we went out to the ruins. Do you happen to know a Roberto Hermosa or a Señor Tatloc?"

"I have not heard of Roberto Hermosa. Señor Tatloc is an archaeologist, yes?" As the boys nodded, Captain Valero went on, "I have heard that some famous archaeologist—I don't know the name—was working at Monte Alban. Perhaps he is Señor Tatloc, but I cannot say for sure."

The police officer paused a few moments, then said, "I am afraid I have not been of much help to you boys. But I wish you luck in your quest. In the meantime, I will keep this note. It will be very good evidence against this overpatriotic, troublesome young group, if they are guilty. I must warn you that they can be dangerous. But you have already found that out."

The Hardys said they would be on guard and report any further trouble to the police. As the brothers walked back to the hotel, they discussed the young zealots. Were they sincere in their motives, or had they perhaps, undercover, been doing a job for the men who were trying to find the Aztec warrior?

"I can hardly wait for morning to come so we can get back to Monte Alban," said Joe. "I have a hunch we're going to get a break in this mystery at last."

"I sure hope that you're right," Frank answered.

The boys passed a food shop which was still open and went inside. Their night's adventure had made them hungry, and they also figured that when Chet woke up, he would be ravenous. They purchased three large *enchiladas* and took them along, together with three bottles of soda.

Chet was still asleep, so the brothers set the food on his night table. They ate their own midnight snack and then went to bed. When the Hardys opened their eyes the next morning, Chet was sitting up in bed reading a magazine, munching his *enchilada,* and drinking soda.

"Hi, you lazy guys!" he said with a pretended look of reproach. "Forget you had an invalid on your hands?"

The Hardys grinned. "Want to ride to breakfast in a wheel chair?" Joe quipped.

Despite his early-morning snack, Chet ate a breakfast of fruit, cereal, eggs, bacon, and two big rolls. The Hardys told him about the warning note, their talk with the hotel manager, and visit to police headquarters.

Their friend gulped. "It's a good thing I didn't know about those guys' reasons for hitting me last night," he said, "or I wouldn't have slept a wink. Things are dangerous enough! You fellows aren't going out to Monte Alban again, I hope."

"We sure are," Frank told him. "Aren't you coming along?"

"Now listen," Chet said, "I'm not chicken, but I don't aim to walk right smack into the middle of big trouble. I got a pretty bad whack on the head, don't forget. You haven't mentioned my goose egg, but believe me, it's plenty sore. Tell you what. Why don't I stay in town and go to the State Museum? I might see something in their collection that would give us a clue."

"Okay," Frank agreed. "See you later."

After he left, Frank and Joe decided to telephone their father and give him a full report. They also wanted to find out how he had progressed with his end of the case of the Aztec warrior.

"Hello, Dad!" said the brothers, taking turns with the phone in their bedroom.

Frank brought the detective up to date on what had happened in Mexico, then Joe asked what luck their father had had.

"Practically none," Mr. Hardy replied. "Sam Radley and I have been over the grounds of the Moore estate several times but haven't found anything to help solve the case." Sam Radley, Mr. Hardy's assistant, was an ace detective himself.

Frank and Joe learned that the only new thing which had been found was another marking on the same tree where the boys had found the carving of the Aztec warrior's head.

"There was a tiny arrow—barely noticeable— near the base of the trunk," Mr. Hardy explained. "Sam and I assume that it might be a guide to something Mr. Moore had buried. We dug pretty deep in several places, but we didn't find anything." The detective chuckled. "We're not giving up, though!"

Frank asked whether there had been any more intruders at the Moore home. The answer was no. "So far as we can discover, there has been no disturbance at the estate, but the police are keeping a close watch. As you boys know, sometimes a criminal will lie low, hoping to discourage his pursuers. When he thinks he's safe, he'll strike again. Well, watch your step, boys. If you turn up anything worthwhile, give me a ring right away."

The brothers promised they would and hung up. After purchasing a booklet on Monte Alban at the hotel newsstand, they set off for the ruins.

In the daylight they could see that the ancient city was even more extensive than they had realized the night before. Of particular interest was an astronomical observatory, around which were grouped a series of mammoth structures containing immense palaces and courtyards.

A court the size of a football field on the far side of the central plaza caught the boys' attention. To reach it they had to climb up and down a series of steps.

"According to this guidebook, the Indians played a game called 'tlachtli'—a combination of our basketball and soccer," said Frank. "They never touched the ball with their hands, only with their shoulders, knees, and feet. The ball had to go through stone rings built high in the side walls."

"Boy, that would really take some doing!" Joe exclaimed.

"Listen to this," Frank went on, "and be glad you didn't live when that game was played. Members of the losing team were put to death!"

"Wow! Sounds more like a battle!" Joe commented. "Well, I've had enough sightseeing. Let's go back to that building where we saw the light last night."

When the brothers reached it, they looked all around for lurking figures, but spotted no one. Quickly they zigzagged to the flat top and scanned the level area below. Nothing extraordinary met their scrutiny.

"If anybody was here," said Frank, "he has certainly packed up and left."

Joe remarked, "Do you suppose those men who tried to attack us came and kidnapped the person?"

Frank did not reply. He had suddenly seen something unusual lying not far away and hurried over to it. Joe followed, and the boys walked around the object—a broken-off chunk of stone. It measured about two by three feet, and was four inches thick. The slab had once been a perfect oblong, but now the upper right-hand corner was gone. On the stone was a carved figure wearing quilted armor, feathered headdress, and ear and lip ornaments. Beneath this was picture writing.

"That's an Aztec warrior!" Joe cried excitedly.

"Exactly!" Frank agreed. "I wonder if it has any significance for us and how valuable it is."

"Say, Frank!" his brother exclaimed. "Maybe this is the valuable find the traveler reported!"

"Could be. But if Señor Tatloc discovered this, why would he have gone away without it?"

"Beats me," replied Joe. "I don't think we should leave it here."

"Right."

The stone, while heavy, was not impossible for the boys to carry. The only thing which worried them at the moment was getting down the steps without damaging the relic. They found it necessary to pause several times in their descent and lay the stone aside.

During one of these periods, Frank took a magnifying glass from his pocket and scrutinized the various symbols on the stone. He smiled. "This thing down in the corner that's almost worn away is a rabbit."

"A rabbit?" Joe repeated.

"I suppose it means that the warrior in this carving was getting ready to offer it as a sacrifice. He has his arms spread out in front of him as if in supplication."

The brothers finally reached the base of the pyramid and started their trek to the car. As they passed the place where Chet had been left unconscious the evening before, Joe remarked, "The guidebook says this is Tomb Number Seven, the one from which so many priceless objects were removed to the State Museum." He chuckled. "Wait until I tell Chet he was buried alive!"

"He'll laugh about it now," said Frank, "but it was no fun being sealed up like a sardine in this place!"

The boys went on to the car. While Joe held onto the unusual stone relic on the rear seat, Frank drove back to Oaxaca and went directly to the museum.

The brothers carried their find into the reception hall and asked for the curator. He came at once, and they showed him the slab.

"We found this at Monte Alban," Frank explained. "We don't know whether it's valuable or not."

The curator, Mr. Louis Juan, asked the Hardys to carry the stone into his office. They laid it on the floor. The man produced a magnifying glass and, kneeling, went over the stone inch by inch.

The boys waited impatiently for his analysis. Mr. Juan, trained in spotting the difference between ancient relics and faked ones, showed no reaction for fully five minutes. Then he stood up and faced his visitors.

"This is remarkable! Absolutely remarkable!" he said.

The Hardys blinked and asked him to tell them why.

The curator explained that the suppliant figure was indeed an Aztec warrior. "He probably was offering a prayer to the war god Huitzilopochtli. That figure no doubt was broken off."

"And what do the rabbit and the little circles around it stand for?" Frank questioned.

"They represent the date. It is the Aztec year 'five rabbit.' That is 1510 according to our calendar."

The Hardys were astounded. "That's even better than we hoped for," said Frank.

The boys were more convinced than ever that this valuable find must have been made by the elusive Señor Tatloc. Would he now be deprived of the credit for having unearthed it? And what had become of him? Had he met with foul play?

Mr. Juan was speaking again. "This relic is outstanding because it proves that there *was* Aztec influence at Monte Alban as far back as 1510. The city there was founded by the

Zapotecs, who were later conquered by the Mixtecs, and whether or not the Aztecs left any impression has been debatable."

"The name Mexico comes from the Mixtecs, doesn't it?" Joe asked.

The curator nodded. "Until now, we have never had any solid proof of Aztec warriors having come this far south. Boys, I congratulate you on uncovering this valuable object."

Frank and Joe insisted that they had merely picked the stone up. "Somebody else discovered it," Frank added.

"And we strongly suspect that it was found by the archaeologist Señor Tatloc," Joe added.

Mr. Juan thought their supposition very interesting. He said that if Señor Tatloc *had* found the stone, he certainly would receive credit for it. The Hardys, already worried about the safety of the archaeologist, felt that now they had an additional reason for finding him as quickly as possible.

"We'd like to locate Señor Tatloc," said Frank. "Can you give us any leads, Mr. Juan?"

The curator shook his head. "That man is like a recluse. We have several very fine relics here which he has sent, but he has never brought any of them himself and refuses to appear in person for any kind of honors."

Before leaving, the Hardys asked the man

whether their friend Chet Morton had visited the museum.

"Is he rather heavy-set?" Mr. Juan asked. When they nodded, he said, "Yes, your friend was here. In fact, he told me proudly that he had made a great discovery!"

# CHAPTER XIII

## *A Charging Bull*

"WHAT's your guess about Chet's discovery?" Frank asked his brother as they hurried back to their hotel. To the brothers' disappointment, he was not there nor had any message been left for the Hardys.

"Chet probably went off to try out another loony idea like that Indian costume bit," Joe said. "When that door opens, be ready for anything!"

As time wore on and Chet did not return, Frank and Joe ceased to joke about it. They became alarmed. There was a good possibility that a member of one of the gangs stalking the boys had captured him. The enemy could be Jack Wayne's kidnapper; the fake detective who had jumped into the boys' taxi; the ringleader, Jimenez; the alley hoodlums looking for revenge; or the overzealous young patriots might have followed Chet and managed to trap him.

A few minutes later Joe said, "It's lunchtime, but I don't feel like eating."

"Same here," Frank agreed. "Perhaps we should get in touch with the police and tell them about Chet."

Joe had another theory about Chet's absence. "He might have seen one of our enemies on the street and followed him."

Frank disagreed. "Chet's a good scout and a big help to us, but I don't think he'd trail a criminal by himself, especially in a country he doesn't know."

As the brothers paced the room trying to make up their minds what to do, the door opened. They heaved sighs of relief. Chet wore a broad grin, so they knew he was all right.

"What's the point of scaring us half to death?" Frank berated him.

The scolding failed to erase the smile from Chet's face. As he unwrapped the package he carried, he said:

"While I was over at the museum this morning, I saw something that gave me an idea. It was an ancient dagger with a serpent's head for a handle. I got to thinking about our Aztec warrior. Mr. Moore was a collector of weapons. Why couldn't the thing we're looking for be a dagger with an Aztec warrior's head for a handle?"

The Hardys stared at their friend. This was good reasoning.

"Chet, I think you've hit the bull's-eye this time," said Frank.

Joe added, "You sure were using your old noggin."

Chet beamed as he finished unwrapping the package. He threw down the paper and held up a dagger.

"Pretty neat, eh?" he asked. *"This* should solve the mystery."

The Hardys examined the dagger eagerly. The blade was made of stone and very sharp, with a wooden handle carved in the form of an Aztec warrior's head. The whole thing measured about fifteen inches.

"This is great, Chet!" said Joe. "Where on earth did you . . . ?"

The door to their room suddenly burst open. Two men raced in and one cried, "Give me that!"

*Wayne's kidnapper and the phony detective!*

The kidnapper wrenched the weapon from Frank's hand and the two intruders backed toward the doorway.

"You can't get away with this!" Frank warned. "We know who you are!"

"You think so?" said the man with the dagger.

"You're Jack Wayne's kidnapper!" exclaimed Joe. He turned to the other man. "And you're the fake detective who got into our taxi in Mexico City!"

The accused men gave a start but made no move to hand over the dagger. Instead, the kidnapper held it pointed menacingly toward the boys until the men were in the hall. As he pulled the door shut, the "detective" warned, "Don't try to follow us or you'll get hurt!"

The Hardys disregarded the threat. Frank whipped open the door and the three young sleuths dashed down the corridor after the fleeing men. The thieves took a back stairway, which the boys had not noticed before. Grabbing the banister, they leaped down two and three steps at a time. But even at this speed, the men they were after were quicker. The pair dashed out into a courtyard. Here they were lost to view amid dense flowering shrubs and trees.

Frank, in the lead, finally spotted the men heading for an open gate to a side street. It was part of an iron picket fence.

"Stop them!" Joe shouted.

Near the gate stood a tall earthenware jardiniere. As Frank drew closer to the men, the kidnapper upended the jardiniere and rolled it directly toward the boy.

Though he, Joe, and Chet managed to leap over it, the momentary delay had been costly. The men had disappeared down the side street. Their pursuers made a minute search but could not locate the thieves.

"Tough luck!" said Joe in disgust.

"All my work for nothing!" Chet complained.

Frank said he would report the incident to the police at once, then he wanted to hear the full story of the dagger from Chet. Ten minutes later they found a quiet table in the hotel dining room where they could talk in private.

"You wouldn't use my Aztec costume," Chet began, "but I thought maybe this dagger would help you. When I was in the costume store, I admired some carvings and got the name of the man who had done them. He lives here in Oaxaca. I went over to his shop later this morning and told him what I wanted. He said he wasn't busy and would make it for me cheap. I thought he'd only carve the head, and I'd have to hunt for the blade myself. But he had an old stone blade that he was going to put a handle on when he had a chance. So he let me have it."

Frank asked, "What made those thieves think it was the real thing? And how'd they find out you were bringing it?"

Joe answered, "I believe we're being shadowed. Those men were listening outside the door. From what little they heard of the conversation they assumed we had the valuable object and took it."

He was interrupted by the waitress. The boys glanced at the menu. "What are *chalutas?*" Joe asked.

She explained that they were small *tortillas*

"Stop them!" Joe shouted

folded over chicken, with peas, carrots, lettuce, tomato, and then fried.

"That's for me," said Chet. "And I'll have some hot chocolate with cinnamon," he added, smacking his lips.

"Make it three," Joe added with a grin. After the waitress had left, Chet continued his story. "It was really great watching that wood carver. Boy, was he fast! I thought maybe I wouldn't have the dagger until tomorrow." Chet heaved a great sigh. "And now I don't have it at all!"

"Never mind," said Joe. "Let's be glad it wasn't the real object Mr. Moore mentioned in his will. But if those thieves think it is, maybe they'll leave us alone."

"And when they learn the truth, they'll come after us again," Frank predicted.

"In the meantime they'll probably try to sell it," said Joe.

Frank remarked that if the local police had put out a net for the kidnapper and the fake detective, officers should be able to pick them up before they had a chance to dispose of the dagger.

"Those thieves are pretty tricky," Joe reminded him. "They probably were a long distance away from here before the police could start looking for them."

The delicious food seemed to put Chet in better spirits. He asked what the Hardys were going to do next.

Frank slapped his chum on the arm. "Right now we're going to follow Detective Morton's clue and look for an ancient dagger with a handle in the shape of an Aztec warrior!"

Chet beamed broadly at Frank. "You mean it? My clue was *that* good?"

"It's worth tracking down," Frank replied. "As soon as we finish eating, I'm going to phone Dad and tell him about your theory."

Chet stuck out his chest so far he almost burst a button off his shirt. All three boys laughed.

They went back to their room and put in the long-distance call. Fortunately, Mr. Hardy was still at home. He was very much interested in the boys' new theory and advised pursuing this angle.

Frank told Mr. Hardy about the discovery of the stone relic and of the Oaxaca curator's great excitement over it.

"Excellent!" the detective said. "Keep going at that rate, and I'm sure you boys will solve the mystery in no time."

With this encouragement, the boys decided to question people along the alleyway into which the dagger thieves had fled. Maybe, Frank said, they could pick up some clues. Since no word had come from the police, the boys assumed the men had not been found.

The three sleuths went down the back stairway and through the courtyard to the cobblestone alley behind it. They walked along slowly toward one of the main avenues, questioning a few people looking out of second-floor windows. None of them had noticed the fugitives. Just before reaching the end of the narrow street, they heard warning shouts.

"Wonder what's up?" said Chet.

A moment later the three boys stopped short. A snorting, angry bull had entered the alley and was thundering directly toward them!

CHAPTER XIV

## *A Matador's Clue*

TERRIFIED, the Hardys and Chet whirled about to flee from the charging bull. They could hear its angry snorting directly back of them.

"We must get to the hotel courtyard!" cried Frank.

He had noticed that all of the open first-floor windows and doors along the alley were barred. There was no chance for the boys to dive to safety through any of them.

The trio had an added moment of panic when Chet stumbled on the cobblestones. But he caught himself, and they went on. By this time the commotion and shouting from people looking out the second-floor windows had spurred the bull on to frantic speed.

Fortunately the gates to the hotel patio were open. The three boys dashed inside, and Frank slammed the gate shut.

They were just in time. The maddened bull

pulled up short, eyed the boys malevolently, then continued on down the alley.

"Boy, I never want to go through that again!" said Chet, dropping to the ground and panting.

The Hardys heaved sighs of relief. Frank said, "I wonder where the bull is now."

"Let's go find out," Joe proposed.

He opened the gate and looked cautiously down the narrow street. The bull was not in sight, but the boys could hear cries of excitement. Quickly they ran in the direction of the shouts. On the way they saw a young Mexican rush from a house. He was carrying a red cloak and a sword.

"He must be a matador!" Joe guessed.

Excitedly the boys hurried after him. The way led to the *zócalo,* where people were running helter-skelter to get away from the animal. Suddenly the angry bull halted, swinging its head from side to side, its horns lowered.

One of the fleeing bystanders spotted the young matador and shouted, "Roberto! Roberto." Others in the crowd called out to him.

Without hesitation, the matador sheathed his sword with the red cloak and walked slowly toward the bull. As it charged toward him, he adroitly swung the cloak and side-stepped the animal. The bull trotted off a short distance, then turned back.

Once more, Roberto walked toward it with

short, steady steps. The animal stood still and glared. Suddenly it lowered its horns again and made a lunge for the matador. Several women screamed, fearful that the man would be gored!

*Roberto gracefully swung his cloak and pivoted to one side. The bull's horns hit the earth and he gave a loud bellow.*

"*Olé! Olé!*" the crowd shouted in praise of the matador's expert move.

As the frustrated beast came toward him, Roberto suddenly pulled out his sword. Frank, Joe, and Chet experienced a sickening sensation —evidently the bull was now to be dispatched. As the crowd watched tensely, a shout came from the edge of the *zócalo.*

A man appeared, crying out, "Do not kill the bull!"

He carried a lariat in his hands. The next moment it snaked out neatly. The immense loop at one end settled down over the bull and was quickly jerked tight. The animal dropped help- lessly to the ground, writhing and snorting.

"Pretty clever!" said Frank.

The beast was pulled to the edge of the *zócalo,* where a truck was parked. The tailgate was down, and quickly the animal was pulled aboard. Then the gate was fastened and the lasso removed from the bull's legs.

Frank, Joe, and Chet exchanged pleased grins that no harm had come to the animal.

Chet remarked, "We sure had a front-row seat to a bullfight that time!"

The man with the lasso explained to the curious crowd that he was driving the animal to a farm outside of town. When the Mexican had stopped for a traffic light, the tailgate had become unfastened and fallen down. The bull had immediately escaped.

"I would have put a ring in his nose and tied him to the side of the truck," the man said ruefully, "but I was hoping to enter him in a bullfight and did not want to mar him."

As the bull's owner drove off, Frank nudged his companions. "Let's go talk to that matador, Roberto, and find out his last name."

The boys pushed their way through the crowd to the center of the *zócalo* where the young matador was receiving congratulations from bystanders.

"Great performance," said Frank, smiling. "By the way, what is your last name?"

The young Mexican grinned. "My full name is Roberto Hermosa Alberto Sanchez."

"What!" Chet's eyes bulged.

The young man looked at him, then said, puzzled, "You seem surprised."

Immediately Joe asked the matador if he knew a Mr. Moore in the States. "No, I don't. I never heard of him."

The Hardys were disappointed. For the second

time their hopes of finding the right Roberto
Hermosa were dashed. They now wondered
whether Hermosa *was* the last name of the man
they sought.

"Do you know an archaeologist named Tatloc?"
Frank questioned him.

Again the matador shook his head. "I spend
most of my time training to be a bullfighter. I
would have no opportunity to come in contact
with a man like that."

Chet now asked, "Is there any shop around
that sells antique weapons?"

"Yes. It's not far away," Roberto replied, and
gave the address.

"Thanks," said Chet. "And good luck to you in
your bullfights!"

As the boys walked away, the Hardys beamed
at Chet. "You're really becoming quite a sleuth,"
Frank said, and added, "If you find a dagger with
an Aztec head on the handle, I'll buy you a good
dinner!"

Chet patted his stomach and grinned. "I'll start
planning what I'll order!"

When the boys reached the shop they found it
to be an amazing place, full of almost every kind
of old-time weapon. Glass cases were filled with
pistols and daggers. Walls were covered with
helmets, suits of armor, and many varieties of
swords and sabers.

A pleasant, middle-aged man emerged from a

rear room. He said the owner was on vacation, but could he help them? Frank told him that they were interested in trying to find an antique dagger with the head of an Aztec warrior on the handle.

The clerk beamed. "You are in luck. One was brought here less than an hour ago."

The Hardys were almost speechless. Chet was grinning broadly. "What did I tell you?" he asked.

The clerk went to the rear room, and came back in a moment with a dagger which he laid on top of a counter. The boys could hardly believe their eyes. The dagger looked just like the one Chet had brought to the hotel!

The stout boy picked up the weapon and examined it. He gave the Hardys a significant look, confirming that it was the same dagger.

"How old is this dagger?" Frank asked the man.

"Quite ancient," the shop clerk replied. "It was found in one of the ruins by two men. The museum didn't seem to want the dagger, they said. I'm sure that it's authentic. Anyway, I paid the men who came in here a good price."

"I'm afraid you've been gypped," said Chet. "That dagger belongs to me. I had it made and it's not old—at least the handle isn't."

The clerk stared in astonishment, then a frightened look came over his face. "If you're right, I've spent an awful lot of my boss's money for nothing!"

"That's too bad," said Frank. "But the story's true. Could you tell us what the men looked like?"

The description that followed exactly fitted that of Jack Wayne's kidnapper and the phony detective. Joe then explained how the boys had been robbed.

"I shall get in touch with the police at once," the man said nervously.

The boys wanted to take the weapon with them, but knew the police would have to examine it first. They told the shop clerk they might return, and he feebly said good-by. The man stood staring after them, chagrined and unhappy.

The boys felt nonplused. Their sleuthing for the afternoon had yielded little, except to prove that the men they were after had quickly realized they had obtained the wrong dagger and sold it under false pretenses to the unsuspecting clerk.

"Here comes the matador!" Joe announced suddenly.

On a hunch Joe walked up to the young man and asked if he knew of anyone else in Mexico having the name Roberto Hermosa.

The matador replied, "Yes, I have heard of such a man. I have never met him, but I understand he lives out near the Tule Tree. He is an authority on Mexican ruins."

## CHAPTER XV

## *The Tule Tree Discovery*

THE Roberto Hermosa for whom they were looking might be an authority on Mexican ruins!
This, thought the Hardys, was certainly a connection with Señor Tatloc!

The boys thanked the matador for his information and returned to the hotel. After consulting
his map, Frank remarked that the Tule Tree was
on the way to the Mitla ruins. "We may as well
keep going and take in the ruins while we're at
it." He added excitedly, "Remember the picture
we found at Mr. Moore's house of the man under
the giant tree?"

"You think maybe you'll find Señor Tatloc
near there?" Chet questioned.

"Possibly. Or at Mitla which is not far from it."

Joe, who had been looking at the guidebook,
asked, "Did you know the Tule Tree is three

thousand years old? It's supposed to be the oldest living thing on the American continent!"

"What kind of tree is it?" Chet asked.

"A green cypress."

"Imagine living all that time and growing bigger every year!" Chet exclaimed.

Joe began to laugh, "Pal, you'd better not live so long!"

The stout boy took the remark with a grin and said, "I'm not worried. The needles you're always putting into me will keep me from expanding."

The following morning Chet decided to go back to the weapon shop and retrieve his dagger. "The police must have finished with it by this time," he said.

"Okay," Frank agreed.

When the boys stopped at the shop, the clerk said they would have to go to headquarters to claim the weapon. He confided that he had not slept a wink all night. "When I told the police about those thieves, they looked at me as if I were stupid. Well, maybe I am. I'm certainly out a lot of money—I know. I'll have to make good."

The three boys felt sorry that the clerk had been duped, but had no solution to offer for his mistake.

"Maybe you'll get a break and make a lot of big sales today," said Frank, as the boys walked toward the door.

"I hope so. I'll have to do something," the clerk

said dolefully. He began to mutter distractedly about "cheats and hoodlums."

The boys slipped out quietly and climbed into the car. After Chet had retrieved his warrior dagger from the police, Frank drove in the direction of the Tule Tree. A few miles beyond town they came upon the tall, stately cypress standing majestically in a park area. The three boys stepped from the car and gazed in amazement at the mammoth trunk.

"It's astounding!" said Joe.

A sign nailed to the trunk said that the tree was one hundred and sixty feet in circumference. Its many branches spread out gracefully over a tremendous distance.

Frank walked around the base of the giant tree. As he gazed upward, thinking how symmetrical the branches were, his foot kicked something. Looking down, Frank saw that he had dislodged a small stone. In the small depression lay a metal object. Frank stooped and picked it up.

"Find something?" asked Joe, who had followed his brother.

"Yes. This looks like a belt buckle."

"Valuable?" Chet asked, grinning.

Frank, intent on scrutinizing the buckle through his magnifying glass, did not answer immediately. "Valuable!" he exclaimed finally. "I'll say! Just look at this!"

Engraved on the back of the buckle was the name Maxli Tatloc. On the face was an ornate engraving of an Aztec warrior standing in the center of a circle formed by a coiled serpent.

The fangs of the serpent formed the initial M and the tail the initial T. Excitedly Frank suggested the meaning. The serpent signified time with the Aztecs. So the warrior, encircled by time, could mean that Maxli Tatloc was a direct descendant of an Aztec warrior.

"Wow-eee!" Chet exclaimed. "That museum curator—back at Oaxaca—sure has competition."

Suddenly the three noticed a Mexican boy of about twelve who had come up silently and stood eying the visitors. Frank smiled and asked him, "Can you tell us something about this tree?"

"For a few pesos I will give you whole history."

Frank dug into his pocket and extracted some coins. The lad's face broke into a flashing grin. He said, "My name is Carlos."

After relating the facts which the boys already knew, Carlos added that the great Spanish conqueror Cortes had rested under the tree on his way to Honduras.

Frank asked the boy if he knew anyone named Maxli Tatloc. "No, I do not. But I have learned in history that in ancient times Maxli was a great Aztec warrior."

His listeners exchanged excited glances. This

bit of information seemed to lend credence to the idea that Señor Maxli Tatloc was the Aztec warrior whom they sought!

"Does anyone around here dig in the ruins?" Chet asked Carlos.

The boy replied with a grin, "Everybody does! We all hope to find treasures and sell them to our government."

"Have you ever heard of a Señor Tatloc?" Joe queried.

"No."

"How about Roberto Hermosa?" Frank asked.

The boy's eyes lighted up. "Yes. Señor Hermosa live nearby. If you wish to see him, drive straight down this road"—he pointed in an easterly direction—"turn left on first street, and stop at house with high white wall around it."

Joe pressed another peso into the boy's hand. "Can you tell us anything about this Señor Hermosa?"

"He is a fine digger," Carlos replied. "He go sometime on long trips with professors."

The Hardys were delighted with this revelation. They hardly dared hope their search might soon be ending, but they had strong hunches it was. The Roberto Hermosa whom they were going to seek out *must* have knowledge of the whereabouts of the Aztec warrior descendant for whom they were looking.

The youngster accompanied the three sleuths

to their car and waved good-by. In a few minutes
Frank drew up in front of the house where Roberto Hermosa lived, and the boys hopped out.
Joe knocked and soon the door was opened by a
plump, elderly housekeeper wearing a black
dress and a flat piece of black lace on her gray
hair.

"Señor Hermosa is not at home," she said in
answer to Joe's question. "He is out at the Mitla
ruins."

"We were going out there. No doubt we'll see
him," Joe went on.

"Perhaps you will," she said noncommittally.
"Mitla is an enormous place, and Señor Hermosa
works in any area which strikes his fancy. I must
warn you about one thing. He has his dogs with
him—and they are not friendly."

Chet frowned. "You can be sure we'll stay away
from them," he said.

Frank smiled. "If we do, we won't be able to
talk with Señor Hermosa—and it's very important that we do."

"I regret I cannot be of more help," the housekeeper said. "Now, if you gentlemen will excuse
me, I must get back to my work."

The boys returned to the car and drove the
rest of the way to Mitla. "That woman was
right—this place *is* immense," said Chet, glancing around in awe. "Boy, look at all those pyramids!"

They parked the car and started to walk.

"According to this guidebook," said Joe, "the architecture of the Mitla pyramids is unique. Every stone that went into the buildings is four inches in length, and they are fitted together so perfectly that no mortar was needed. They have lasted since about the year A.D. 70!"

The site contained four huge major palaces and a number of smaller ones. These opened off a central court.

"Look at all those steps!" Chet remarked. "I'm going to call Mexico the country of steps."

The Hardys were more interested in the angular stone doorways, some of them opening into tombs from which skeletons and treasures had long since been removed.

As the three sleuths neared one of the buildings, Chet looked in dismay at the low doorway. The only possible way to enter was to crawl. This prospect did not please him.

"You fellows go ahead," he suggested. "If you see anything worthwhile, give a yell and I'll come."

The Hardys gave their chum a look of pretended disgust. Joe said, "What kind of sleuth are you?"

"I'll stay out here and look around for Roberto Hermosa," Chet announced, unruffled.

Frank and Joe dropped to their knees and pulled themselves through the low opening. The roof of the tomb was not much higher, and they were unable to stand up.

Joe, in the lead, advanced a few feet. As he was reaching inside a hip pocket to pull out his flashlight, he heard a menacing snarl. Was this one of Hermosa's unfriendly dogs or a wild animal?

Joe started to back up hurriedly and bumped squarely into Frank. Before either boy could reach the exit, suddenly terrific growling and yapping started in the tomb. The next second an animal's long fangs sank into one of Joe's legs!

## CHAPTER XVI

# Stunning News

JOE cried out in pain. Instantly a man's voice yelled in Spanish, "Down, Sol! Down!" The animal released its hold on the boy's leg.

A bright light was beamed on the Hardys, who were still trying to back out of the tomb.

"You're only boys!" cried the voice behind the light. "I thought you were ruffians! I am sorry! Are you hurt?"

Frank and Joe did not reply. They kept scrambling backward until they were outside.

"Wh-what happened?" Chet asked in concern.

Before the brothers could answer, a man emerged from the low doorway. He was followed by two handsome but fierce-looking shepherd dogs.

Without speaking, the Mexican examined the teeth marks on Joe's leg. Seeing that the skin had not been broken, he looked relieved.

"I hope you will forgive Sol. I keep the dogs with me for protection. He felt you boys were going to harm me. I was in an inner room of the tomb and did not hear you come in."

Frank looked directly at the Mexican and asked, "Are you Señor Roberto Hermosa?"

"Why, yes, I am. How did you know?"

Frank explained about stopping at the man's house and that they had come down from the States searching for a person by that name. "You won't mind if we ask you some questions?"

"Not at all."

"Did you know a man named Jonathan Moore who lived in Bayport?"

"No, but I heard a friend of mine mention his name many times."

Frank inquired if the friend Hermosa had just mentioned was Señor Tatloc.

The Mexican's eyes opened wide. "Yes. And how did you know that?"

The young sleuth did not answer the question directly. Instead, he asked whether the two men were business or personal friends.

Roberto Hermosa laughed. "I guess you might call us both," he replied, "although I do not see much of Señor Tatloc any more. A few years ago we used to go on digs together, then suddenly he seemed to want to work by himself."

"Do you know where he is now?" Joe spoke up.

Hermosa shook his head. "But I will be very

glad to help you find him, if it is important. You spoke of a Mr. Moore. Who is he?"

Frank pulled the various prints from his pocket and showed them to the Mexican. He instantly recognized Señor Tatloc in the picture, but said he did not know the other man.

"That's Mr. Moore," said Frank. "He mentioned a Roberto Hermosa in his will, and we think you are the one."

"*I* am in his will!" the Mexican exclaimed.

"It is still a puzzle to us," said Joe. "My father is a detective. He and my brother and I were commissioned to find a descendant of an Aztec warrior and also an Aztec warrior object."

As Hermosa fairly jumped in amazement, the boys introduced themselves.

"Then you're young detectives," said Hermosa. "Well, maybe you can explain a few things to me. I told you I take my dogs everywhere with me for protection. The reason is that during the past two weeks I have been mysteriously attacked several times. Men I have never seen before seize me and threaten my life if I won't tell them where the valuable Aztec warrior is."

The Hardys and Chet gave one another significant looks. Were Hermosa's attackers part of the same gang who had been harassing the boys regarding the Aztec warrior?

"I have no idea what these men are talking about," the Mexican continued. "Every time I have insisted they have the wrong man, and they finally release me. Can you enlighten me about these Aztec warriors?"

"That's one thing we are trying to find out," Frank replied.

Roberto Hermosa seemed to be a forthright and interesting individual. The Hardys felt it safe to tell him the provision in Mr. Moore's will.

Suddenly the Mexican gave the boys a big wink and laughed. Then, to their surprise, he told them that Señor Tatloc had lent Mr. Moore a valuable and ancient heirloom which Tatloc planned to will to a museum. Apparently the North American had promised to return it within a given period, and was to keep the whole matter a secret to avoid any publicity and possible theft.

"I do not know what the article was, however," Hermosa concluded.

"The only hitch was that one or the other of the men might die before the time was up," said Frank. "In this case, Mr. Moore passed away first."

Roberto Hermosa said, puzzled, "Evidently I was elected to be the intermediary. I was to identify Señor Tatloc, who does claim to be a direct descendant of the Aztecs. But what I cannot understand is the reference in the will to the Aztec warriors. Have you any ideas?"

"Yes, but only theory," Frank replied. "Since

Mr. Moore was a weapons collector, we think the object is an ancient weapon, with part of it, perhaps the handle, representing an Aztec warrior. Did Señor Tatloc ever mention such a thing?"

"No."

Hermosa was thoughtful for a moment, then he said, "The men who attacked me must know about Mr. Moore's will or have other information about the warrior. How could they have got it?"

The Hardys gave him a quick but complete account of the mystery from its start.

The Mexican frowned. "I do not like being mixed up in this affair," he said. "But since I am, I will question other men who dig in the ruins. They may have seen Señor Tatloc recently."

"Thanks," said Frank. "By the way, was there a great Aztec warrior in ancient times named Maxli?"

"Indeed there was! And you will be interested to know that Señor Tatloc is a direct descendant of that great Aztec warrior."

The Hardys and Chet could hardly conceal their excitement. There was now no doubt in their minds that Maxli Tatloc was the man for whom they were looking!

Frank showed the belt buckle to Hermosa. "We found this near the Tule Tree," he said. "Do you think this belongs to your friend?"

"Yes, that is Señor Tatloc's buckle. I knew that he had lost it. He was very much upset because he prized it highly. He would be pleased to know it has been found."

Frank smiled. "It would give us great pleasure to present it to Señor Maxli Tatloc."

The Hardys said they would keep in touch with Roberto Hermosa, and asked that he telephone them if he picked up any clues to the whereabouts of the archaeologist. They all shook hands and the boys went to their car.

As they drove along, Joe suggested they report their latest findings to Mr. Hardy.

When they reached the hotel Frank put in the call. Mr. Hardy praised the boys' productive sleuthing and then said he thought they should advertise in the large Mexican newspapers for any information leading to Señor Maxli Tatloc.

"We'll do it right away," said Frank.

As soon as he had said good-by, the Hardys and Chet set off for the office of an Oaxaca newspaper. They were told that the advertisement would appear in the following morning's edition.

Next day the boys hurried downstairs for an early breakfast. Frank paused to buy a paper. A headline splashed across the front page made him catch his breath. He hurried to catch up with his companions, crying, "Look at this!"

The headline read:

WELL-KNOWN ARCHAEOLOGIST MAXLI TATLOC
BELIEVED KILLED IN FALL FROM MOUNTAIN

# CHAPTER XVII

## *Treacherous Trail*

AFTER Frank, Joe, and Chet had recovered from their initial shock, they read the article which gave the details of Señor Tatloc's probable death. Three North American tourists—William Kimmer, Ronald Naylor, and Burt Humphrey—had reported seeing Señor Tatloc in a wild, mountainous area.

"The minute the men saw him topple over the cliff," the article went on, "they rushed to the edge. But there was no sign of Tatloc anywhere below.

"Kimmer telephoned the authorities. Naylor phoned the story to this paper. A rescue party was sent out at once, but the archaeologist has not been found. It is assumed that Tatloc fell into the river at the foot of the canyon, was killed, and his body swept away."

The boys reread the article before speaking. Finally Chet said, "It's terrible news. This will change your plans, won't it, fellows?"

"It looks that way right now," Frank conceded. "Before we do anything more, I believe we should phone Dad."

As soon as they finished breakfast, Frank put in the call. Mr. Hardy, who fortunately had not yet left the house, was stunned by the news. "This changes the whole aspect of the case," he said. "Does the newspaper article say that Tatloc *fell* off the cliff?"

"Yes."

"It's just possible he was shoved off," said the detective. "You boys have plenty of evidence now that certain people will let nothing stand in their way to obtain the Aztec warrior object. One of their big stumbling blocks would be Tatloc."

"This gives a pretty grim twist to the case," Frank commented. He then asked his father what the boys should do next.

Mr. Hardy took so long to answer the question that Frank thought the connection had been cut off. He finally said, "Hello? Are you there, Dad?"

"I'm still here," came the answer. "I was thinking—it just occurred to me that this whole story of Tatloc's death may have been trumped up."

Frank was astounded. "You mean those American tourists are fakes?" he asked.

"That's my suspicion—there may not be any tourists from the States with those names. I suggest you check at once with the Mexican Tourist Department. You remember they took up one part of your tourist card when you entered the country. In that way, the department has a record of everyone coming into Mexico."

"Great idea, Dad! We'll do that!"

Frank repeated the conversation to Joe and Chet, then put in a call to the Tourist Department in Mexico City. The official to whom he talked promised to look up the information and call him back as soon as possible.

While they were waiting the boys began to speculate: If the story *were* false, what was the reason behind it?

"Maybe it's some kind of scheme the gang planned," Chet suggested.

Frank agreed. "Yes, that could be—to force Señor Tatloc to disclose his whereabouts."

Joe jumped up from the chair. "Could be this whole story was faked just so we'd give up the case!"

Again the boys became silent for several minutes. Finally Chet sighed and said, "I wish we'd hear from the Tourist Department. This suspense is killing me!"

At that moment the phone rang. Joe answered. He listened, then thanked the caller and hung up.

"That settles it!" he exclaimed. "No American tourists with those names have entered Mexico."

"Wow!" Chet cried. "Then the whole story *is* phony!"

"This gives me a new idea," said Frank. "I think we should work on the theory that Tatloc was kidnapped."

"Kidnapped!" Joe explained. "By whom?"

"By the Aztec warrior gang!"

"Sure!" Joe agreed excitedly. "We can try to get a lead on those tourists from the police. Then we can scout the area where Tatloc was supposed to have disappeared."

"We'd better report all this to Dad," Frank suggested.

Mr. Hardy was waiting for his son's call. "Good work, boys!" he said. "Let me know if you find out anything about those tourists."

"Will do, Dad. By the way, any developments on your end of the Aztec mystery?"

"Very little," the detective answered. "We made another exhaustive search of the Moore grounds, however, and came across something of possible significance."

"What is it?" Frank queried eagerly.

His father said that on various trees near the house, he and Sam Radley had found tiny arrows carved into the trunks at ground level. Some of the markings were even hidden by grass. "As yet Sam and I haven't figured out what they mean. But we'll keep working at it on this end. Good luck to you boys!"

Mr. Hardy said good-by and Frank immediately phoned the police. He was told that the story of Tatloc's fall had come in by phone. Frank relayed to the other boys their newest assignment to trail the kidnapper.

"Good night!" cried Chet. "Now you expect me to tangle with kidnappers who push people over cliffs?"

"Suit yourself," said Frank. "The thing that bothers me is how we can ever trail these kidnappers without a single clue."

Joe suggested, "If the mountain area *is* the place where Señor Tatloc was kidnapped, he was taken some distance away. But we might pick up some kind of lead to the place where he's being held."

"You're right," Frank agreed. "If searchers are still looking for him in the canyon, we'll probably have a better chance of picking up an untrampled clue on the mountain."

Once more the boys consulted their map. The region in the newspaper account lay in a northeasterly direction from Oaxaca. The Hardys and Chet set off in the car and soon found themselves on a narrow, twisting road which led higher and higher up the mountain, its peak lost in the clouds. There was a scattering of native huts. Now and then the boys caught glimpses far below of a rushing stream which they assumed was the one into which Señor Tatloc was supposed to have fallen. Near the base of the mountain, tall evergreens grew thickly, but higher up these thinned out and gave way to shrubs and bare rocks.

"If Señor Tatloc was around here, there must be ruins," Chet remarked.

"It doesn't mention any on the map," Joe pointed out. "But he may have made a discovery."

"Could be," Frank conceded.

For some time they had passed no more mountain huts and in a little while the road ended.

"Now what?" Chet asked.

Frank again studied the map. Then he said that the spot for which they were aiming was directly above them. "From here I guess we climb."

Chet groaned loudly. "What's the use of all of us going?" he asked. "If there are kidnappers around, somebody ought to guard the car."

"Okay, you do it." Frank grinned. "I'll turn this bus around, so it's heading down. Chet, if you hear us give our special birdcall whistle, drive back to town fast, and get the police."

"Suits me," the stout boy agreed.

Frank and Joe started up the craggy mountainside, each wondering if they were on a futile mission. The brothers were beginning to doubt that Señor Tatloc would have come to this spot.

Also, it occurred to the Hardys that they might be walking into a trap! They stopped for several minutes to discuss the matter.

"Dad suggested this trip," Frank argued, "and we have a job to do."

This thought spurred the boys on, and they began to climb faster. Chet, watching from below, lost sight of his friends as the clouds enveloped them.

"It's chilly up here," said Joe, "and visibility's poor."

"That should keep us from being spotted," Frank remarked.

The Hardys finally reached the summit, which was flat for several hundred yards. They crossed it and looked down into the canyon. Through spaces between the drifting clouds they could see the almost barren mountainside with the rushing stream below.

"Nobody could have survived a tumble down there," said Frank. He shuddered slightly.

The boys walked around the plateau but could see nothing to give them a clue. They kept walking for some distance along the top until they came to a place where it started sloping downward.

Suddenly Joe grabbed Frank's arm and pointed at the earth. "Footprints! And all mixed up!"

"Must have been a scuffle here!" Frank stated. The Hardys, excited, followed the prints.

They found some indicating that a man evidently had been dragged away!

"These prints are easy to follow," said Joe. "Come on!"

He and Frank slipped and slid on the treacherous gravelly soil through which a natural path dipped and rose. At an especially slippery, jagged section the footprints disappeared completely. Nevertheless, the boys climbed over the huge outcropping and came to the path again. Here the footprints resumed.

Instinct warned the Hardys to become more cautious. They almost tiptoed along, keeping a sharp lookout for any signs of the presence of human beings.

About a hundred yards farther on, the boys suddenly stood stock-still. Just ahead of them was a crude thatched-roof structure built close against the mountainside.

"Imagine living here!" said Joe in a whisper.

"That crude hut looks newly constructed," his brother observed. "We may have reached the end of our trail, Joe!"

Moving with extreme caution, the young detectives proceeded. Since no one seemed to be around, they moved up to the hut and looked through the open doorway.

Inside, on the floor, lay a man bound and gagged!

## CHAPTER XVIII

## *Vaquero Attack*

ALTHOUGH the face of the prisoner in the hut was distorted by the gag in his mouth, Frank and Joe were sure he was the man they were seeking.

The Hardys hastened inside. Joe quickly untied him, and as Frank pulled out the gag he asked, "You are Señor Maxli Tatloc?"

The lean, gray-haired man sat up and nodded, apparently unable yet to speak. Joe noticed a gourd hanging at the back of the hut. "Maybe there's water inside," he thought, and dashed over to get it.

Returning to the archaeologist, he said, "Perhaps a drink of this will help."

The man, with a grateful look, drank thirstily. Then Señor Tatloc heaved a great sigh and with the boys' help stood up.

"*Gracias,*" he said weakly. "Thank fortune you have come."

"Are you sometimes called the Aztec warrior, Señor Tatloc?" Frank asked.

The archaeologist looked startled. "Yes, I am. How do you know? Who are you?"

"Frank and Joe Hardy. We've come to help you," Frank told him.

"Then get me away from here as quickly as possible," Señor Tatloc said in a stronger voice. "We must all get away from here before those bandits return!"

Frank and Joe were eager to question the man further, but realized that this was not the time to do it—he was barely able to walk or talk. Explanations on both sides must wait.

Though the Hardys chafed at the necessary delay, they said no more. Supporting the archaeologist between them, the trio started back along the ridge, intending to follow the natural trail down the mountainside.

They had not gone a hundred feet when three tough-looking Mexican men they had never seen before appeared from behind an outjutting rock. At the same instant, three lassos snaked out toward Frank, Joe, and Señor Tatloc!

Two of the lariats landed around the shoulders of Frank and the archaeologist, and were quickly drawn tight. Joe managed to dodge the one meant for him, and put up a game fight against the man who had just tried to capture him. The two rolled over and over on the ground as Frank and Tatloc's captors roared loudly with laughter.

Frank was on the point of giving the whistle signal, but stopped himself. Right now it might only lead to further danger for him and the others. He struggled violently to get free, but, with both arms pinioned tightly to his sides, his efforts were futile. He was infuriated to see the stranger getting the better of his brother, but the Mexican was apparently a trained fighter. In a few minutes he overpowered Joe and tied him up with the lariat.

The strangers, who avoided calling one another by name, soon had all their prisoners tightly roped. The men kept laughing raucously, and finally one said in Spanish:

"We are vaqueros, but not roping cattle this time. We came to get this prize fish." He indicated Señor Tatloc. "When we saw you two boys climbing up the mountain, we went back to our car for our ropes in case we needed them. Lucky we did."

"Why do you want to capture us?" Frank demanded.

The vaquero laughed. "In your country do you not punish anyone who tries to take a prisoner away?"

"But you have no legal right to be holding this man," Joe spoke up angrily.

"That is a matter of opinion," came the quick reply. The man shrugged. "I thought you two boys were little fish, but I believe now maybe you are a big fish too. And we caught you with something better than a butterfly net. You cannot get away!"

The vaquero stopped speaking, called his friends to his side, and talked in whispered tones. The boys could not distinguish any of the conversation. From the men's scowls, however, it was evident they were having an argument. Finally the leader announced, "We have decided to take only the biggest fish with us. You boys will remain in the hut."

Frank and Joe gritted their teeth in desperation. They were so tightly roped that even though they might eventually free themselves, precious time would be lost and Señor Tatloc probably would have been taken far away!

"At least we could go to the police and give a description of these vaqueros," Frank thought.

His hopes waned a moment later when the boys were told that the man with whom Joe had fought would remain as guard.

"I'm going to try our whistle," Joe decided in desperation. "If Chet can hear me, he'll go for the police."

But before Joe could whistle, the guard came up to the Hardys, whipped handkerchiefs from his pocket, and gagged the brothers. Frank and Joe were pulled into the hut, while the archaeologist was led off by the two vaqueros.

The Hardys writhed in anger and discomfort. Now they could neither move nor talk! All they could do was consider their predicament and try to figure out a method of escape. Also, they were greatly worried about Señor Tatloc.

The boys' thoughts also turned to Chet. What was he doing? When the Hardys did not return, or signal within a reasonable time, surely he would become extremely concerned. Would he drive off and get the police?

In a little while the guard came over to where Frank lay on the earthen floor and stared down at him. "If you do not yell out, and answer my questions," he said, "I will remove the gag."

Without waiting for a response, he yanked out the handkerchief and asked, "Where is the Aztec warrior?"

"Why, you just took him down the mountain," said Frank.

"Oh, I don't mean that old fossil," the guard replied. "You know well what I mean. Where is the valuable item you boys are going to turn over to Tatloc?"

Despite the gravity of the situation, Frank could have yelled for joy. The gang not only had not found the Aztec warrior object but did not know that it probably was still in the States.

"I wish we knew," Frank replied coolly. "Suppose you tell me how you and your friends happen to know about this warrior business."

"That is none of your affair," the man answered. "You and your father are very clever, I'll admit. You have hidden that Aztec treasure well, but we'll find out where it is." Suddenly the man's eyes grew fiery. "We'll worm the information out of that crazy archaeologist!"

"How—if he won't talk?" Frank asked.

The guard laughed. "That old man prides himself on being a direct descendant of an Aztec warrior. Well, we'll try some of those ancient Indians' torture methods on him. He'll talk!"

With that, the guard thrust the handkerchief back into Frank's mouth. The Hardys exchanged frantic looks. Their own situation was bad enough, but Señor Tatloc was in real danger! Somehow they must get free, and rescue him!

The hours wore on and dusk began to fall. From his pockets the guard pulled out a couple of *tortillas* and a bottle of water. He sauntered outside, leaving the door open. He seated himself in front of the hut, leaning back wearily against it.

The man ate the food greedily and drained the contents of the bottle. From where the Hardys lay, they could watch him clearly. Suddenly the man's head dropped forward and within seconds he was snoring loudly.

At once Frank and Joe began working vigorously to loosen the lariats. The knots were tight, however, and the boys' efforts proved futile.

Exhausted, they lay back to catch their breaths. Suddenly the Hardys saw a stout figure glide into the hut.

*Chet!*

The brothers' hearts pounded excitedly. Chet tiptoed over to them and yanked out their gags. Then he produced a pocketknife and quickly cut the knots and unwound the lariats.

Frank and Joe could have hugged him for joy, but there was no time to take one extra moment for anything but escape. The three boys rapidly wound the ropes around the still-sleeping guard. As the man started to wake up, Frank gagged him with a handkerchief. By this time, the man was fully awake, but could do nothing except glare malevolently at his captors as they dragged him inside the hut.

"I brought a couple of flashlights," said Chet, pulling them from a pocket. "Frank, lead the way!"

"Chet," said Joe, "in return for rescuing us, I promise not to needle you again—"

"Ever?" asked Chet.

Joe grinned. "Well, not until tomorrow anyway."

Frank called over his shoulder, "Chet, you really came through in the clutch. My reward to you will be a dinner with all the food you can eat!"

"It's a deal." Chet grinned.

The brothers' hearts pounded excitedly

As the boys carefully picked their way down the mountainside, Chet explained that he was sure something had gone wrong. "I didn't want to take time going for the police, so when I couldn't stand the suspense any longer, I grabbed flashlights and started up here. Boy, what a climb! Did you find out anything about Señor Tatloc?"

When Chet was told what had happened, he whistled in dismay. "You found him and then before you could question him those vaqueros ruined your chance of solving the case!"

"I don't think our chances are ruined," Joe spoke up. "When the police get hold of that guy up in the hut, I'll bet he'll talk."

The boys returned to Oaxaca as quickly as they dared drive on the winding roads. Though disheveled and dirty, they went at once to police headquarters and reported what had happened. The officer in charge promised to send police out to the mountain spot at once and bring in the vaquero.

"You young men had better go to the hotel and get some rest now," he said kindly. "Tomorrow morning I'll let you know what the prisoner reveals. In the meantime, please do not say anything about the fact that Señor Tatloc is alive. It must have been the gang that captured you who gave out the false report about the archaeologist's death. If they are not aware that we know the truth, it may be easier to round up these criminals."

The Hardys and Chet promised to keep the information to themselves and went to a restaurant. Ravenous, they ate a hearty meal. Then they walked directly to the hotel and dropped into bed, exhausted.

The next morning Frank, awake first, greeted the others with the remark, "I think I know where Señor Tatloc was taken!"

# CHAPTER XIX

## *Island Prisoner*

"WHERE?" Joe and Chet exclaimed in astonishment.

"Lake Patzcuaro!" Frank told them excitedly. "Remember the reference those vaqueros made to butterfly nets? That's what the fishermen there use."

"You're right!" Joe declared. "Let's go!"

Chet too was eager for the trip. "Even if Señor Tatloc isn't there, I'd like to see those fishermen who use nets different from any others in the world."

Patzcuaro was a long way from Oaxaca in a northwesterly direction. The boys decided to start out early and stop for lunch at Taxco, which was on the way. At eight they phoned the police. The guard at the hut had been jailed but refused to answer any questions. There was no other news.

By nine o'clock they were on the road. They

reached Taxco around lunchtime and parked in the large, tree-shaded *zócalo*. Cobblestone streets rose up the steep mountainsides surrounding it. Facing the public square was a very handsome old stone cathedral. The other three sides were lined with attractive shops and restaurants.

As the boys walked around before selecting a place to eat, they noted that many of the shops sold silverware. "Taxco is noted for its silver mines and skilled silversmiths," said Frank as they paused before one window. "Boy, look at that figure!" On display was the statue of an Indian carrying a large pouch from which he was sowing a handful of corn seeds.

As the boys walked on, they saw several artists, seated on canvas stools, painting the scenes around the *zócalo*. The boys stopped to watch a red-bearded man who was wearing a bright-blue smock. He was sketching a little boy pulling a tiny burro.

The artist looked up at the visitors and smiled. "You are from the States?" he asked in English. When they nodded, he went on, "I lived there once myself, but I found so many fascinating things down here to paint I never went back!"

"Do you specialize in figures?" Joe asked him.

"Pretty much," the artist replied. "By the way, my name is Don Hawley." The boys shook hands and introduced themselves.

Mr. Hawley continued talking as he went on

with his sketching. "I don't believe this picture will be much good. I am feeling sad. I read in the newspaper that a man whose portrait I painted was killed."

Mr. Hawley added that the man was a great archaeologist. Hearing this, Frank asked quickly, "Was he, by any chance, Señor Tatloc?"

"Why, yes. I guess you read the account, too."

"We did," Frank replied, then asked, "Where is the portrait of Señor Tatloc?"

"In my studio. It is a living likeness. Come, I'll show it to you. I'm too upset to do any more work today." He put a few pesos into the hand of his boy model and told him to return the next day.

On the way to the studio, Joe asked Mr. Hawley about the archaeologist. The artist said that the man was an extreme contrast to his nickname. "Señor Tatloc was a very peaceful person, yet his friends at the university affectionately called him 'the Aztec warrior.'"

"Was his only hobby going on digs for relics?" Frank queried.

"Just about," the artist replied. "Señor Tatloc had one of the most extensive and enviable collections of Aztec weapons and other artifacts in the world. Many had been handed down through his family for hundreds of years. Upon his death he wished the pieces to go to the State Museum.

They're locked up in a bank vault since he had no permanent home."

The Hardys and Chet acted casual, but were excited at the new information. Tatloc and Moore did have the common interest of collecting weapons. By this time they had reached the studio, which opened directly off the pavement of a side street. Inside, they were confronted by a life-size figure on canvas. This was indeed the man the boys had met in the hut!

"The painting is great!" said Frank. Grinning, he added, "I wish I had money to buy it."

"Oh, it's not for sale," said Mr. Hawley. "This picture was commissioned by a man very much interested in the State Museum. The portrait is to hang there, but Señor Tatloc requested that this not be done for another two years. He didn't say why."

The Hardys glanced at each other. Two years more would round out the five-year period after which Mr. Moore was to return the Aztec warrior object to its owner. Was there a definite tie-in between the two dates?

The boys drew closer to the portrait to inspect it in detail. Señor Tatloc was arrayed in a gorgeous Aztec costume, and in his hand he held a dagger with an obsidian blade and handle, which was carved in the form of a plumed serpent. It was studded with turquoise.

"Have you ever seen Señor Tatloc's weapons collection?" Frank asked Mr. Hawley.

"No, and he was rather secretive about it. In fact, Señor Tatloc remarked at the time we started this portrait that he wished it were possible for it to be painted two years from now. At that time he would have received a much more interesting dagger."

"What does that one look like?" Joe asked excitedly.

"Señor Tatloc did not say."

The boys thought they knew the answer! The dagger must be the Aztec warrior object! Frank asked Mr. Hawley, "Did Señor Tatloc ever mention a man named Jonathan Moore?"

"No."

After looking at several other fine pictures, the boys thanked the friendly artist and then said good-by. As they walked down the street toward a restaurant, Chet remarked, "That was a lucky break. You fellows just about have this mystery wrapped up, don't you?"

Frank shook his head. "I wish it were true, Chet. We don't know where the living Aztec warrior is, and we don't know where the missing dagger is hidden."

After lunch Chet took the wheel of their rented car. As he drove along, he caught up to a bus crowded with men, women, and children, carrying strange-shaped bundles and baskets from the market. The overflow of passengers was seated on the roof of the bus, clutching live chickens and dogs. One boy even had a baby goat.

The sight of barnyard creatures on a bus set the three boys to laughing. Suddenly a chicken wriggled loose from under its owner's arm. The hen squawked loudly as it flew through the air and landed *smack* on the windshield of the car. Startled, Chet let the car swerve, narrowly missing a deep ditch at the side of the road as he jammed on the brakes.

"Good night!" he cried, as the stunned chicken fell into the road.

By this time the owner of the hen, a stout woman, had yelled for the bus driver to stop and was now climbing down a ladder on the outside of the vehicle. Reaching the pavement, she ran back to the boys' car and began to wave her arms in anger at Chet.

He sat mute as she picked up the hen, which was dead, and demanded in voluble Spanish that Chet pay for the finest egg layer in her flock.

"You'd better do it," Joe advised with a grin.

"But it wasn't my fault!" Chet remonstrated. "Anyway, if I have to pay her for the hen, it's mine. But what'll I do with a chicken? It's probably good eating, but how could I cook it?"

At this, both Hardys burst into laughter. Their hilarity infuriated the woman. She held the hen by its feet and waved it in the air with one hand. With the other she made irate gestures at Chet, threatening to have him arrested.

Completely abashed and a bit frightened, Chet pulled out his wallet, removed a bill, and handed it to the woman. Her reaction was a surprise. Dark looks changed to a broad smile and with a mighty heave the woman threw the hen into the car. Then, waving the bill triumphantly, she ran back to the bus and climbed the ladder. As the vehicle started off, she blew kisses at the boys!

The Hardys roared with laughter as Chet, red in the face, sat staring at the chicken. "What are we going to do with this?" he asked.

"Like to stop for a picnic?" Joe needled him.

Just then Frank noticed a little girl standing not far away in a field. Evidently she had heard the commotion while playing near her farm home which was not far away. Without a word, Frank picked up the hen. He walked over to the child and handed it to her.

"You take this home," he said, smiling.

*"Gracias,"* the little girl said, and ran off across the field.

The boys drove on and toward evening reached the quaint village of Patzcuaro. They checked into a small hotel on one of the narrow streets. After washing up, they lost no time in trying to find a clue to Señor Tatloc's whereabouts. As they questioned people in the hotel and on the street, they showed the pictures of the archaeologist. No one had seen the man in town. Disappointed, the boys went to bed.

"I can't get the reference to butterfly nets out of my mind," said Frank, just before they all went to sleep. "Tomorrow morning let's go down to the lake and question fishermen."

This procedure brought results. Three men said they had seen the stranger in the pictures. He was in a public launch heading for the island of Janitzio. The boys could see the hilly island, far out in the lake. Atop it was a huge statue of Morelos, the priest who headed the victorious revolution of 1810.

At once Frank inquired about renting a launch to take them over to the island. He was directed to a small dock where a boat was waiting. The boys quickly climbed aboard, and soon the craft was chugging across the water.

The boys were fascinated as they watched fishermen swing their huge nets, which resembled giant butterfly wings, and gracefully let them down into the water. As the nets were raised again, thousands of tiny fish the size of sardines squirmed and flopped inside.

The pilot of the launch told his passengers it took years to become skilled at using these nets.

"What do they do with such tiny fish?" Joe inquired.

"They are taken to Janitzio, dried on mats in the sun, and sent mostly to Mexico City. They are considered a great delicacy."

As the boat drew near the island, the boys saw that along the beach was a row of crudely hewn dugouts which belonged to the fishermen.

"They're unusually wide and long compared to the ones we sometimes use for camping trips," Frank said.

Here and there on the beach were groups of women busily mending fish nets. Their dexterity amazed the boys.

Frank made arrangements for the pilot to wait, and they began their sleuthing. First, Frank showed the pictures of Señor Tatloc to the women, who pointed up the hilly street just beyond. It was a narrow, cobblestone road lined with shops and houses. In front of them stood huge poles between which the giant butterfly nets had been stretched.

Again Frank showed the pictures, this time to some men, who also pointed up the hill.

"Now we're getting some place!" said Joe, starting off at a fast pace.

"Hold on!" Frank advised. "I don't see any policemen around, and we may run into trouble. I think we should get a couple of husky men to go with us."

The other boys agreed. Two fishermen, with pleasant faces and bulging muscles, were chosen.

When Frank explained the situation, the men looked startled and one said:

"Kidnappers on our island! Zapato and Pancho will be glad to help you search."

The group trekked up the hill, inquiring at each shop and house, but they met with no success. At the top the road turned left. The Hardys decided that the searchers would divide their work.

Frank chose the most distant point and sprinted ahead of the others toward the last house on the street. All the doorways were open.

"Nothing looks sinister or suspicious around here," he thought.

Nevertheless, Frank inquired at each dwelling. As he came to one where no one seemed to be at home, he was suddenly yanked inside and the door closed.

Frank's cry for help was cut off by a gag being thrust into his mouth. The next instant his arms were pinioned and a huge fish net wound round him. He was then thrown into a corner of the one-room shack, where a pile of fish nets was tossed over him.

Frank churned with anger at being caught off guard. There was silence for several minutes, then Frank heard a man say, "What can I do for you?"

"Can you identify the man in this photograph?" It was Joe speaking!

There was a slight pause, then the man answered, "Yes, I saw this old fellow. He was with two other men. They went down to the lake. An American boy was following them."

"Thank you very much," said Joe. "We'll go right down there and look for them."

Silence followed. As Frank lay helpless, he knew that Joe and the others had left.

## CHAPTER XX

## *A Secret Unearthed*

THE silence was broken by Frank's captor starting to taunt him. "You thought you were so smart, but I have outwitted you this time."

The man's voice was not familiar, so Frank knew he was neither Jack Wayne's kidnapper nor the phony detective.

The man went on, "You and Señor Tatloc will never be released until you tell us where the valuable Aztec dagger is. You fooled my friends once with an imitation."

Frank felt as if he would suffocate beneath the fish nets. As he shifted uncomfortably, Frank suddenly became aware of another human being lying next to him. The prisoner must be Señor Tatloc! Frank's heart pounded excitedly, but quickly his hopes of rescue or escape faded.

Meanwhile, Joe and his companions had reached the shore. Their launch was still there.

Joe rushed up to the pilot. "Did my brother

leave here in another boat?" he asked quickly.

"No. I haven't seen him."

Joe looked at Chet and the two fishermen, Zapato and Pancho. "Frank must have been captured! I'll bet he's in the hut where that man told me Frank went down the hill!"

He turned and hurried back up the incline, with the other three following him.

It did not take the group long to reach the hut. The two men inside looked startled as the searchers walked in boldly.

"Where's my brother?" Joe demanded.

"What do you mean?" asked one of the men.

By this time Joe's and Chet's eyes had become accustomed to the semidarkness of the hut. One of the men was the phony detective!

Frank, hearing the commotion, made a desperate attempt to move and managed to thump the earthen floor once with his feet.

"He's here!" Chet exclaimed.

At this, the two thugs made a rush for the doorway. Zapato and Pancho grabbed them, while Chet blocked the entrance.

Joe was already throwing aside the heap of fish nets and now set about freeing the two prisoners. He released Frank first, then the archaeologist. The elderly man looked exhausted.

"Thank goodness you have come!" he murmured.

Gently Frank and Joe carried Señor Tatloc out to the street.

"I'll be all right," he said. "Last night I heard my kidnappers talking about you boys and your famous father. You must be excellent detectives to have traced me here!"

"They certainly are excellent detectives!" said Pancho. "But this one!" he exclaimed, glaring at his prisoner. "He lives here—among us. But he's a bad one. I should have known right away he would be mixed up in this evil thing." He gave the prisoner a shake. "What shall we do with these two bad ones?"

"We must take them to the police in Patzcuaro," Joe replied. "Could you go there with us?"

"We will be glad to," said Zapato.

The island residents along the way watched in open-mouthed amazement as the prisoners were marched down to the launch.

The pilot stared in disbelief. "You caught the kidnappers?" he cried out.

"We sure did," Chet answered.

The prisoners were sullen and refused to talk. Señor Tatloc, however, told the whole story of his abduction. He had suspected the mountaintop held the ruins of an ancient temple and had gone there to investigate.

"I was captured and taken to the hut where

these same two men tried to force a secret from me. Then you boys came and were taken prisoners. How did you escape?"

"Chet Morton rescued us," Joe replied.

Señor Tatloc said he had been dragged down the mountainside, put into a car, and driven to Patzcuaro. "These men"—he pointed to the prisoners—"threatened to torture me if I didn't tell them what they wanted to know. But I refused."

The prisoners' eyes flashed with hate, and the phony detective snarled, "Don't think you're safe! You haven't captured our friends yet, and they're going to get what they want!"

"The police will take care of that," said Frank.

As soon as the group reached Patzcuaro, they went to police headquarters and the prisoners were taken into custody. The fishermen said they must return to the island. Frank tried to pay them for their work, but they refused the money.

"First time in my life I ever captured a crook," said Zapato with a wide grin. "It has been a pleasure meeting you brave boys." There was a round of thanks, then the two islanders left.

When the officer in charge heard that the phony detective was wanted in Mexico City and Oaxaca, he telephoned the police in both cities. After a while he came back to the boys, smiling broadly.

"I have excellent news for you," the officer

said. "The leader of the gang, Pedro Jimenez, has been taken into custody in Mexico City."

"Pedro Jimenez!" Señor Tatloc exclaimed bitterly. "He was my guide and helper for many years!"

The officer interrupted to say he had further information. "The man who kidnapped your pilot," he told the Hardys, "is also in custody in Mexico City. The other two vaqueros were jailed in Oaxaca after their friend talked. They gave the false report about Señor Tatloc's death. The whole gang has now been caught."

"What a relief!" said Señor Tatloc. Chet and the Hardys grinned their satisfaction.

Before leaving police headquarters, the boys learned that Jimenez had confessed his guilt. He had been working for a very wealthy, dishonest collector who would go to any length to get what he wanted. The hoodlums in Mexico City and the young zealots at Monte Alban were not part of Jimenez's gang.

The Hardys thanked the police for all their help, then left with Chet and Señor Tatloc for the hotel. Here Frank made the elderly archae-ologist lie down to rest while the boys explained about Mr. Moore's directive to the Hardys to find the Aztec warrior and return his property to him. Briefly, they outlined their adventures since undertaking the case, including their meeting with Roberto Hermosa.

The archaeologist listened intently, and when Frank and Joe finished, he said quietly:

"Now I will tell you the story of the Aztec warrior object. One day, about six months ago, after discharging Jimenez—he had become very surly—I was in a hotel room talking on the phone with my good friend Mr. Moore. I caught Jimenez eavesdropping. I'm afraid he overheard enough of our conversation to have planned the theft of a dagger—a priceless heirloom which has been in my family nearly a thousand years. My relatives bicker about it. They think the weapon should be sold and the money divided among them. I don't agree, mostly because it belongs to me. For this reason I have always kept its whereabouts a secret."

As Señor Tatloc paused, Frank asked, "You lent the dagger to Mr. Moore, but no one knew this except you two and Pedro Jimenez?"

"That's right."

Chet asked a bit impatiently, "What does the weapon look like, Señor Tatloc?"

"The blade is made of obsidian and is still sharp. The handle, beautifully carved in the shape of an Aztec warrior, is inlaid with jade and turquoise and rubies.

"Three years ago when Mr. Moore came down here looking for old weapons, I showed him my collection. He begged me to sell him the dagger. I told him I didn't think it should be taken out of Mexico, and said that I planned to will it to the State Museum. Finally he persuaded me to let him enjoy having it in his possession for a while. Knowing that he could be trusted to take good care of the dagger and return it within the five-year period we agreed upon, I let him take it."

"Did Mr. Moore ever tell you where he kept the dagger?" Joe asked.

"No, he did not tell me. Do you mean it hasn't been found?"

"Not yet, Señor Tatloc."

The archaeologist looked stunned. "I shouldn't have let him talk me into borrowing it. But he was very persuasive—in fact, he offered a check to finance a museum field expedition. We arranged to have a guarded stipulation in both our wills for the return of the relic."

"I'm sure we'll locate it," Frank said. "But the dagger is certainly well hidden. Mr. Moore must have known—or suspected—that thieves were after it."

"Where does Roberto Hermosa fit into the picture?" Joe asked.

Señor Tatloc answered, "To prevent anyone's learning I owned the object mentioned in Mr. Moore's will, we chose Roberto Hermosa to make the identification of me. Roberto knew that I had lent Mr. Moore an heirloom, but did not know what the object was. I am deeply grieved to hear of Mr. Moore's death, and I must say that he took every precaution to keep our secret. During the telephone conversation that Jiminez overheard, I told Mr. Moore that as soon as I received the dagger I was going to present it to the State Museum. I was afraid that some of my greedy relatives might get hold of it. I would like to go to Bayport with you and help search for the heirloom."

"Great!" Frank said.

He told the archaeologist about the pictures they had found among Mr. Moore's slides. "One was taken in a garden."

"Oh, yes, that was at a house outside Mexico City. Mr. Moore rented it for a month."

"Another picture shows you in costume," said Frank.

Señor Tatloc smiled. "A celebration was held near the Pyramid of the Sun. Some of the university professors requested that I take part in the celebration. I did not wish to, but they insisted. I wore a very old costume I have and Mr. Moore took my picture."

"By the way," Joe asked, "were you at that pyramid the other day? We thought we saw you there."

"No, I wasn't," the archaeologist replied.

Frank asked him, "Did you find a relic at Monte Alban and leave it there?"

"Yes, Frank. I uncovered an ancient slab with an Aztec warrior and a date—five rabbit—carved on it. The slab was too heavy for me to carry away. While I was waiting for a friend to come and help me, I went up to that mountain to look for the ruins of a temple. That's when the kidnappers took me prisoner."

"We found the slab," said Joe, "and took it to the State Museum. We told the curator we thought you had uncovered it."

"And that's not all we found," Frank said. "This belongs to you." He handed over the belt buckle and told him about picking it up.

Señor Tatloc stared in amazement, then said, "Thank you, boys, for all you have done."

Frank put in a call to his father, who was both amazed and pleased to hear what had happened. "Your hunch paid off, Dad. And now we're ready to come home. Señor Tatloc will accompany us."

"Very good," said the detective. "I'll send Jack Wayne right down."

The boys and their passenger drove to Mexico City the next day. There they took off in the Hardys' private plane. Jack Wayne was generous in his praise. "I'm certainly glad my kidnapper is behind bars!" he said.

The morning after they arrived in Bayport, Mr. Hardy, Sam Radley, and the lawyer, Mr. Weaver, took the boys and their guest out to the

Moore estate. Frank and Joe were eager to examine the tiny arrows which the two detectives had found on the trees.

After seeing them, Joe spoke up, "Dad, is it possible that this circle of arrows represents a boundary to limit the area where we are supposed to search? And that the Indian's head is the starting point?"

"You may have hit on the answer!" Mr. Hardy exclaimed.

Though many sections within the circle had already been dug up, work was started on other sections. Suddenly Mr. Hardy disappeared inside the house but soon came out, smiling.

"I may have a clue," he said. "A tile pipe leads out from the cellar and under the lawn. It doesn't seem to have any use. I poked a stick in as far as I could, but didn't find anything. Boys, will you look around for a plumber's snake? We'll run it into the pipe and see if we can hit anything."

Frank, Joe, and Chet rushed off to the garage, part of which housed a tool shed. Inside, they found the long wire tool, hurried to the cellar, and inserted the snake. About twenty feet underground it came to an obstruction, but the boys were unable to budge it.

"Let's dig up the ground at the end of the pipe," Joe urged.

Excitement mounted as the searchers rushed outdoors. They judged that the pipe's end lay under a large spiraea bush. Frantically they dug it up, then spaded out the earth beneath.

Soon Frank's pointed shovel uncovered the end of the pipe from the cellar. It was plugged with a concrete disk. Unsuccessfully the boys tugged at it. Using a chisel, they finally yanked the disk loose.

Inside the pipe lay a package with a waterproof canvas cover. The boys pulled it out carefully. Attached to the end which had faced the cellar was a metal ring.

"Mr. Moore probably had a long pole with a hook on the end of it to grab the ring so he could drag the package out to the cellar," said Frank.

Chet groaned. "I saw one in the garage."

Frank lifted out the package and handed it to Señor Tatloc. "I think you should have the honor of opening this. Don't you, Dad?"

"Without question," his father agreed.

"I think we'd better go into the house to look at the contents," Mr. Weaver advised, leading the way.

The package was laid on Mr. Moore's desk. Fingers trembling, Señor Tatloc opened it. Revealed was the Aztec warrior weapon! Its carved handle, inlaid with turquoise and jade, and the warrior's headdress of fiery red rubies glittered in the light.

"This is the handsomest piece of its kind I've

ever seen!" Mr. Weaver exclaimed. "Señor Tatloc, you indeed own something priceless that a gang of thieves would certainly go to great lengths to steal."

The archaeologist smiled. "It wouldn't have done anybody any good if it had not been discovered by the Hardys and Chet. Without them, my secret might have remained one forever and a precious relic lost to Mexico. Hundreds of years could have gone by before this object was discovered. I am very grateful to you all."

As the boys, somewhat embarrassed, were searching for an answer, Mr. Weaver spoke up. "There are a great many other people who are going to be thankful as well—the beneficiaries of Mr. Moore's will. They'll be able to collect their inheritances now."

Frank and Joe, though pleased that the mystery of the Aztec warrior had been solved, were already wondering what their next adventure would be. Very soon another exciting case— THE HAUNTED FORT—would be a real test of their ingenuity and courage.

Chet Morton was overwhelmed by all the praise and excitement. "Señor Tatloc and Mr. Weaver," he burst out, "when Frank and Joe solve a mystery, they usually have a party with plenty of good food. Let's all go to the Hardys' house and give Señor Tatloc a chance to taste some good old U.S.A. cooking!"